ENVY
THE DEAD

MYSTERIES BY ROBERT J. RANDISI

Hitman with a Soul Trilogy
Upon My Soul
Souls of the Dead
Envy the Dead

The Miles Jacoby Series
Eye in the Ring
*The Steinway Collection (aka
Beaten to a Pulp)*
Full Contact
Separate Cases
Hard Look
Stand Up

The Nick Delvecchio Series
No Exit from Brooklyn
The Dead of Brooklyn
The End of Brooklyn

The Gil & Claire Hunt Series
Murder is the Deal of the Day
The Masks of Auntie Laveau
Same Time, Same Murder

The Joe Keough Series
Alone with the Dead
In the Shadow of the Arch
Blood on the Arch
East of the Arch
Arch Angels
Back to the Arch

The Dennis McQueen Series
The Turner Journals
Cold-Blooded

The Rat Pack Series
*Everybody Kills Somebody
Sometime*
Luck be a Lady, Don't Die
*Hey You, with the Gun in Your
Hand*
*You're Nobody til Somebody
Kills You*
I'm a Fool to Kill You
Fly Me to the Morgue
It was a Very Bad Year
You Make Me Feel So Dead
The Way You Die Tonight
I Only Have Lies for You

The Auggie Velez/Nashville
Series
*The Honky Tonk Big Hoss
Boogie*
*The Last Sweet Song of
Hammer Dylan*
The Festival of Death

Jimmy Spain Poker Series
The Picasso Flop
The Judgment Fold

Stand Alone Crime Novels
The Disappearance of Penny
The Ham Reporter
Curtains of Blood
The Offer
The Bottom of Every Bottle

Collections
Delvecchio's Brooklyn
The Guilt Edge

ROBERT J. RANDISI

ENVY THE DEAD

Book 3 of the Hitman With A Soul Trilogy

Down & Out Books
3959 Van Dyke Rd, Ste. 265
Lutz, FL 33558
www.DownAndOutBooks.com

Cover art and design by JT Lindroos

ISBN: 1-943402-55-8
ISBN-13: 978-1-943402-55-7

To Marthayn,
My very own Voodoo Queen.
You put a spell on me.

"Envy the dead, we will yearn for our death
Silence is the peace for the one I search...
...there is no time for remorse
Just envy the dead"

—Tristitia

PROLOGUE
Philadelphia, PA
3 years ago

"Father Patrick?"

"Yes?"

"The Monsignor is ready for you now."

Father Patrick looked up at the huge crucifix above the altar, unclasped his hands, hastily crossed himself and stood.

He followed the younger priest from the church to the rectory and to Monsignor Genova's office.

William opened the door, but did not go in. Instead, he stood aside and said, "I'm sorry, Father."

"Wha—" Father Patrick started, but young William hastily walked away, head down and eyes averted.

"Father Patrick?" the Monsignor's voice called from inside. "Are you coming in?"

"Yes, Monsignor." He entered the room, wondering exactly what William was sorry for.

"Have a seat, Father."

The Right Reverend Monsignor Vincent Genova sat behind his desk, his bald head gleaming in the light from the overhead fixture. He was wearing his black hassock with red buttons down the center.

"Monsignor," Patrick said, "what did Father William mean—"

"William was supposed to tell you I was ready for you," Monsignor Genova said, "and that was all. Did he say something more?"

"Well, no—"

"You young priests," the older cleric said, shaking his head.

Patrick did not lump himself in with William as a "young" priest, since he was a full ten years older and William was literally a year out of seminary.

"He said nothing, Monsignor."

"Yes, well," Monsignor said, sitting back in his chair. He made a steeple of the fingers of both hands. Patrick always expected the man to recite that old, "this is the church, this is the steeple, open the door and see the people," nursery rhyme when he did that. "I'm afraid I have some bad news for you, Father."

Patrick was afraid of this. He closed his eyes and waited.

"Bobby Abbatello committed suicide last night."

Patrick's eyes popped open. That was not quite the bad news he'd been expecting.

"Wha—but how?"

"He leaped from his family's twelfth-floor balcony."

"Sweet Jesus!"

He expected Monsignor to take him to task for that, but the older man showed some uncharacteristic understanding of the situation.

"Are they sure—"

"It was suicide?" Monsignor asked. "Yes, the young man left a note."

"A note?"

"Yes," Monsignor said. "The note absolved you of any culpability, Father...of any kind."

Patrick covered his face with his hands.

"Did you hear what I said, Father?"

"I heard you, Monsignor."

"You don't seem at all relieved to be absolved—"

"Relieved?" Patrick snapped, cutting the older man off abruptly. "Should I be relieved that a twelve-year-old boy has taken his own life, Monsignor?"

"Well, uh, no, of course not," Monsignor said, "but by the same token there will be no charges against you—"

"I couldn't care less about that!" Patrick snapped. "That poor boy. My God, that poor family!"

"That poor family, Father," Monsignor said, "was ready to string you up by your entrails."

"They thought they had cause," Patrick said.

"And now they know they had none," Monsignor said, "but that doesn't seem to have appeased them."

"I beg your pardon?"

"According to the police," Monsignor said, "they still want your head, Father."

"Well…" Patrick said, but his mouth was too dry to continue.

"And since the Abbatello family is still the largest crime family in Philadelphia, the Diocese thinks it only prudent to move you…"

ONE
New Orleans, LA

Sangster was sitting on the porch of his house in Algiers Point, Louisiana, ruminating on two problems.

The first was on the chessboard in front of him. He was deep in a game with his neighbor, the ex-sheriff of Jefferson Parish, Ken Burke, only Ken had to leave in the middle of it.

"It'll give you time to consider your position," Burke had said, "which is pretty well—ah, kind of hopeless—oh, let's just say you're pretty well fucked. But you figure it out. I'll be back later."

Burke left, and Sangster stared at the board.

But at the moment he was thinking about his other problem: should he stay in New Orleans? It had taken him a few years to establish himself here, find his house and make friends with Ken Burke. But on a couple of occasions he'd been found by people who knew him from his old life, when he made his living as a hitman. It's what he was before he woke up one morning and discovered he suddenly had a soul.

He didn't really want to move on and find a new home. But he also didn't want to bring any more death to New Orleans. So if he stayed, he'd have to make sure nobody ever found him, again. That meant keeping low—very, very low.

He looked up from the board and saw a man coming up the walk. He wore a leather bomber jacket, a black shirt, jeans, and the collar of a Catholic priest.

"Hello, Patrick."

"Sangster."

Patrick mounted the porch. Sangster pointed to the chair usually inhabited by Burke. On occasion, though, since he became friends with Patrick a few months earlier, the priest would also come around for a game. Or a beer.

"Blackened Voodoo in the fridge," Sangster said. "Get two?"

"I'll be right back," Patrick said, and went into the house.

When he came out, he sat in the chair across from Sangster and handed him one of the beers. Then he looked down at the board.

"Wow," he said.

"Yeah, I know," Sangster said. "I'm fucked."

Patrick took a swig from his bottle.

"Got a minute?"

"I've got several," Sangster said, sitting back. He welcomed the respite from thinking about his two problems. "What's on your mind?"

"I'd like to tell you a story."

"To what end?"

"I may be askin' you for your help," Father Patrick said. "And I mean, the kind of help you can offer with your special skills."

Sangster had killed a rival hitman inside the Holy Name of St. Mary's Catholic Church right in front of Patrick several months earlier, so the priest knew all about his "special skills."

"Okay, then," Sangster said. "Tell me a story..."

"It goes back three years, when I was at St. Paul's in Philadelphia..."

Sangster listened intently, didn't ask any questions, and didn't speak until Father Patrick stopped talking.

"We need more beer," he said. He held a hand out to Patrick, "I'll get them."

He went inside to the fridge, collected two more bottles of Blackened Voodoo and took them outside. Patrick knew all of Sangster's sins, so Sangster was not prepared to judge the man in any way. Besides, if everything Patrick had told him was true, he was innocent.

"Okay," he said, sitting back down.

"What, no questions?"

"What should I ask you, Patrick? If you had an illicit sexual liaison with a twelve-year-old boy? I believe you did not. Let's move on."

"Thanks," Patrick said, "but obviously his family doesn't feel the same."

"Why are you worried about his family?" Sangster asked. "Mafia crime families have fallen by the wayside. It's all Russian and Columbians now."

"That may be the case," Patrick said, "but Bobby's father isn't the type to give up so easily."

"Are we talking about getting his family back in control in Philadelphia or getting revenge for his son?"

"Probably both, but I'm more worried about the second."

"You think he's coming after you?" Sangster asked.

"I don't think he's forgotten about me in three years," Patrick said. "This is my third post in that time, tryin' to stay ahead of Abbatello and his family."

"Excuse the question, Father," Sangster said, "but why not change professions if you were going into hiding?"

"I can't give up my vocation, Sangster," Patrick said. Although Sangster used the name "Richard Stark" while living in Algiers, both Ken Burke and Father Patrick had found themselves in a position to learn his real name, although neither knew exactly what he used to do.

"Not even if it gets you killed?"

"I think I'd rather die than not be a priest anymore," Patrick said.

Sangster stared at the man. Patrick was in his late-thirties, and Sangster had the feeling that he was a late-comer to the priesthood. He wondered what Patrick had done before entering the seminary, but he had never asked.

"If you're going to be that stubborn about it," the ex-hitman said, "it might turn out that way."

TWO

"Why are you telling me this?" Sangster asked.

"I was in the French Quarter yesterday. I went to Jackson Square; I wanted to see St. Louis Cathedral."

"You've been here a few months," Sangster observed. "You haven't seen the Cathedral yet?"

"I was staying away from it," Patrick said. "I thought—well, I didn't want to be recognized."

"In Jackson Square?" Sangster said. "All you had to do was wear some silver make-up and a Day-Glo jacket you would've blended right in."

"I wish I'd thought of that."

"You're not telling me..."

"I think I recognized somebody I know," Patrick said, "but I don't know if he saw me."

"Who was it?"

"A guy named Vincent Napoli—they called him Vinny Nap."

"Was he in the Abbatello family?"

"He was a hanger on," Patrick said. "Always tryin' to get in, you know?"

"What was he doing when you saw him?"

"He was watchin' this little black boy tap dance," Patrick said, "and sippin' somethin' from a cup through a straw."

"Probably one of those stupid-flavored margarita

drinks. So what are you thinking, Patrick?"

"I think Vinny might have been sent here to look for me and got distracted by the kid dancin'," Patrick said. "Or he's here because he's on the run from somebody, and if he saw me he'd see it as an opportunity to get back in. Either way, I'm fucked."

Sangster knew Patrick was upset because, in the short time they'd been friends, the only time he'd heard him use profanity was when he wasn't wearing his clerical collar.

"What do you want me to do, Patrick?"

"I know I don't have the right to ask you to do anything, Sangster," Patrick said.

"Just spit it out, man."

"I need to know if Vinny saw me," Patrick said. "If he's even still in New Orleans."

"And if he did and he is?"

Patrick shrugged.

"I'll have to cross that bridge when I come to it," he said.

"So that's all you want?"

"Yes. Oh, I see. You thought I was going to ask you to kill him?"

Sangster shrugged and stared at the chessboard.

"I know you don't do that, anymore," Patrick said, "just like I—" He stopped short.

Sangster looked at him.

"Look. All I need is to know what Vinny Nap knows."

"I'm not a detective," Sangster said.

"You know people," Patrick said, "and you know how to get things done. You can find him."

"How will I know what he looks like?"

Patrick reached into his pocket and brought an old newspaper clipping.

"That's him, in the background."

Sangster accepted the picture. Whatever the article was about, it wasn't included, only the picture.

"This Jimmy Abbatello?" Sangster asked, indicating the man in the forefront of the photo.

"That's him."

Further back Vinny Napoli was looking on, probably hoping he'd get into the photo somehow. As it turned out, he did.

"Do you have more photos than just this one?" Sangster asked.

"I do," Patrick said. "In fact, I have quite a collection of the Abbatello family."

"Why?"

Patrick shrugged. "Just keepin' track, I guess."

"No better photos of this guy Vinny?"

"No," Patrick said, "but I could go with you to the Quarter and point him out."

"No offense, Patrick, but I think you better stay away from there for a while." He indicated the newspaper photo, which was still in the priest's hand. "That is, at least until we know what's going on with this guy."

"Then you'll help me?"

"I'll take a look at this guy and see what I can see," Sangster said, "but no promises after that."

"Okay."

Patrick put his empty beer bottle down and stood up.

"Thanks, Sangster."

"Don't thank me, yet," Sangster said. "And if you

want me to do anything after this I might have to ask some more pointed questions."

"Understood." He started down the steps from the porch, then turned and indicated the chessboard. "And you really are, uh, screwed."

As Patrick walked away, Sangster realized that after several months he still didn't know the man's last name.

THREE

Vinny Nap went back to Jackson Square twice since the day he thought he saw Patrick Carnahan. He'd been watching the little nigger kid with the fast feet dance for quarters, when he turned his head and he could've sworn he'd seen Patrick. But when he looked for him he'd either disappeared or he was never there.

Vinny was in New Orleans because he was trying to get away from winter in Philadelphia. He'd hit a Pick 3 at Parx and decided to spend the money on a trip. He'd only been in New Orleans a few days and Jackson Square was like no place he'd ever seen before. There was the silver guy standing on a box and only moving like every fifteen minutes or so to change position, the dancing kid, the palm and tarot card readers, the artists. Walking around the streets he'd never seen so many corner bars that sold flavored margarita drinks, and he'd also never seen so many ATM machines. Jesus, they were almost on every corner. If he'd ever been able to figure out how to pry those suckers open, this would've been the place to make a shit-load of money!

But maybe he *did* have a way to make some money and to get on the inside all at the same time.

Patrick Carnahan.

He knew the Abbatello crime family had fallen on hard times and was trying to get back its place in

Philadelphia, but he also knew that Jimmy Abbatello was still looking for Patrick Carnahan, the priest who diddled his kid and drove him to suicide.

Vinny knew Carnahan. They grew up in the same Philly neighborhood. He'd only caught a glimpse, but he was pretty damn sure it had been him. It was kind of a shock to think of Paddy being in New Orleans, but then he himself was in New Orleans, so why not?

Paddy and Vinny had gone their separate ways as they got older—Vinny into a life of petty crime, and Patrick into the service of God. Later, he came back to Philly and Vinny was surprised to find that he was a Catholic priest. The Paddy he knew as a kid never gave any sign he was leaning in that direction. In fact, after Paddy got out of Catholic grammar school, he never went back to Sunday Mass, as far as he knew.

But they'd never really been friends, so Vinny never had the chance to ask Paddy about his turn to the Church. Vinny was too busy trying to get accepted into his own religion—the Mafia. The Abbatello's had run South Philly for years, and Vinny had wanted in ever since he was a kid. But he'd never been able to prove himself worthy. Maybe now was his time.

If he could spot Patrick Carnahan again, and pass the info on to Jimmy Abbatello…

So he went back to Jackson Square the next day, and the day after that, hoping to spot him again.

And he had a gun on him, just in case he got a clean shot. Killing Father Patrick for Jimmy Abbatello would definitely get himself accepted into the family. The Abbatellos may not have held the power they once had, but Vinny had faith that they would be able to take care of the Russkies and the Spics. And when they took the power back, he wanted to be there when they did.

He sat at a table in front of a café, smoking a cigarette and drinking an Abita beer. For two hours he had been watching the people stroll in and out of the park, stopping to gawk at performers or have their fortunes told.

"Would you like something else?" the waiter asked him. "It's almost lunch time."

He looked at the waiter, then at the menu in the window.

"What's that?"

"Which one?"

"The muff-muffy—"

"Muffaletta?"

"Yeah, that."

"It's a New Orleans special, but it's actually an Italian sandwich."

"Is that right?"

"It's got ham, capicola, salami, cheese—"

"I'll have one," Vinny Nap said, "and another beer."

"Coming up, sir."

A couple of more hours wouldn't hurt. Maybe Patrick would come walking by.

FOUR

Sangster met with Father Patrick at the Holy Name of St. Mary Catholic Church on Eliza Street.

When he had been looking for answers about his soul he'd gone to many churches, and eventually walked into St. Mary's. Sangster never found out the exact count, but there were many Catholic and Baptist churches in Algiers. Sometimes called "The Cathedral of the West Bank," this particular church was probably the most impressive single structure in Algiers. It was also the first Roman Catholic church in New Orleans.

It was where he first met Father Patrick.

Patrick led him past the front steps of the church to the rectory and inside.

"Where's your boss?" Sangster asked.

"The Monsignor is in Rome for a conclave," Patrick said. "He'll be gone weeks."

He led Sangster through the rectory until they reached Patrick's bedroom. Sangster had never been there before. It was spartan, with a bed, a dresser, a desk, a chair and a lamp.

"Wow," Sangster said, "you guys really do take a vow of poverty."

"Did you think we were secretly rich?"

"I think the Catholic Church is not so secretly rich,"

Sangster said. "Obviously it doesn't trickle down to its foot soldiers."

"Foot soldiers," Patrick repeated, thoughtfully. "I like that." He turned to his dresser. "Why don't you have a seat on the bed. I've got a scrapbook here."

Sangster sat on the single bed, found the mattress very firm. He watched as Patrick opened the bottom drawer of the dresser and took out a book.

Patrick put the book on the desk. "Have a look. I'll go and ask Mrs. Cox to make some sandwiches for lunch."

"Sounds good."

Patrick left the room as Sangster seated himself at the desk and opened the scrapbook. For some reason, the priest had a collection of news clippings about Philadelphia's dominant crime family, the Abbatellos.

But the articles seemed to have a theme—the downfall of the Abbatello family. Each successive page and article seemed to describe how they were losing power as Russians and Columbian gangs moved into the city.

There were many photos of Jimmy Abbatello, the young head of the family. The last article in the book described Jimmy as being forty-one years old, the patriarch of a "dying entity."

Sangster assumed Patrick thought if the family fell fast and hard enough, they'd forget about him.

Patrick reentered the room carrying a tray with sandwiches and beer on it.

"Mrs. Cox made two po' boys."

"Great."

The priest set the tray down and sat on the bed with his sandwich. They each started to eat.

"So whataya think?" Patrick asked.

"Seems to me you've been hopin' they'd have so much trouble they'd forget about you."

"That's pretty much it," Patrick said. "Only if Vinny's here lookin' for me, then I doubt that's what's happened."

"And if he's not here looking for you?"

"Then I don't want him telling them he's seen me," Patrick said. "It might remind them about me."

"I don't think they're about to forget that their son killed himself or anything to do with it."

"I had nothing to do with it," Patrick said, tightly.

"I told you, I believed you."

"Good."

They chewed and washed the food down with swigs of Abita.

"Patrick, how long have you been a priest?"

"About ten years."

"So you were a late starter?"

"Oh, yeah."

"What did you do before the priesthood?"

Patrick took time with the question by drinking some more beer.

"Sangster," he said, "I've never asked you what you did before you came to New Orleans."

"But you have a pretty good idea."

"I do, yes," Patrick said. "But I didn't ask."

"True."

"My past—before the seminary—it's not somethin' I'm proud of. And maybe someday we'll talk about it. But not today. That is, unless you're makin' it a condition of helpin' me."

"No," Sangster said, "no conditions. I'll go into the French Quarter and see if can find this guy."

"And if you do?"

"I'll find out what he's doing here."

They finished their po' boys and beer, and then Patrick walked Sangster to the door.

"Tell Mrs. Cox the sandwich was great."

"That'll please her. When will you go to the Quarter?"

"Tomorrow."

"Aren't you, uh, trying to keep a low profile these days?"

"I am."

"Then maybe you shouldn't—"

"I can't stay home and do you this favor," Sangster said.

"Maybe you should take help," Patrick said, "you know, to watch your back, just in case?"

Sangster turned on the doorstep to look back at Patrick.

"That might not be a bad idea."

"You got somebody in mind?"

Sangster smiled. "I think we both do."

FIVE

Sangster knocked on his neighbor's door the next morning with coffee and beignets in hand.

"You went to Café du Monde and came back?" Ken Burke asked.

"No," Sangster admitted, "I got them at that place that opened up a few blocks from here."

Burke leaned forward and sniffed at the open bag.

"Well, beggars can't be choosers. Come on in."

Burke led the way into his kitchen, where they sat at the table and tore the bag open.

"To what do I owe this fine continental breakfast?" the ex-sheriff asked.

"I have a favor to ask."

"So ask."

"Actually," Sangster said, "I'm doing a favor for Father Patrick, and I need a little help."

"Patrick's okay," Burke said, and then added, "for a priest. What's his trouble?"

Briefly, Sangster outlined the problem Patrick was having, and then explained what he was planning on doing to try to help him. He left out the part about the priest being accused of abuse.

"Correct me if I'm wrong," Burke said, when Sangster was finished, "but after what happened a few months ago, weren't you going to keep a low profile and not go into the Quarter so much?"

"I haven't been there in three months," Sangster pointed out.

"But you intend to go now."

"Just for a short time," Sangster said, "but first I need you to use some of your local connections."

"To do what?"

"Find out if a guy named Vincent Napoli is registered in any New Orleans hotel."

"In the Quarter?"

"Anywhere. He was spotted in Jackson Square, but he could be staying anywhere."

"And if I locate him? What are you gonna do then?"

"Talk to him."

"Just talk to him?"

"Just talk."

Burke bit into a beignet, washed it down with coffee.

"So, what do you say?" Sangster asked.

"I'll put the word out," Burke said, "but next time I want the real thing from Café du Monde. If you're going to the French Quarter anyway, come back with the real thing."

"Well," Sangster said, "that was the other thing."

"What other thing?"

"When I do go to the Quarter I'll need a, uh, partner."

"A partner?"

Sangster nodded.

"Somebody to watch my back."

"You want me to recommend somebody?"

"No," Sangster said, "I want you to strap on the old Colt and back me up."

Burke frowned.

"Is this gonna be messy?"

"I don't think so," Sangster said. "While I'm concentrating on this guy Vinny Nap, I'll need somebody to check and see if anybody is concentrating on me."

In his old life as a hitman, Sangster would have trusted himself to do both jobs. But he wasn't that guy anymore. And he trusted the old sheriff who, he knew, could still do the job.

"So you were kidding about the old Colt," Burke said.

"Oh yeah," Sangster said, then added, "I'm sure you have a much newer gun you can carry."

"How's a Glock sound?"

"Perfect."

SIX

Detectives Telemaco and Williams of the NOPD stared at each other across the expanse of the back-to-back partner's desks.

"I don't like them," Telemaco said.

"What's not to like?" Williams said. "They're partners' desks."

"Actually, they're not," Telemaco said. "A true partners' desk is one piece of furniture, not two set back-to-back."

Williams frowned.

"What are you, some kind of desk expert?"

"My sister buys antiques," Telemaco said.

"That figures."

"Why?" Telemaco said. "You sayin' my sister's an antique?"

"I didn't say that," Williams said. "Look, forget it. You want your old desk back? Fine. I'll have it brought up from the—"

"Relax, partner, relax," Telemaco said. "I didn't say that. The desk is fine. I just wish we could do something about the face I have to look at all day long."

"Har-har."

"What've we got for today?"

"We got a missive from the Philadelphia Police."

"A missive?"

Williams glared at his partner. "It's my new word for the day."

"Okay, okay," Telemaco said. "What's this 'missive' say?"

"They've been keepin' tabs on a low-level crumb named Vinny Napoli, also known as Vinny Nap."

"These wiseguy nicknames are so old hat," Telemaco said. "It's funny now."

"Well," Williams said, "he was seen at the airport in Philly, gettin' on a plane that was comin' here."

"So? Maybe he's on vacation?"

"They're askin' us to keep an eye on him and let them know what he's up to."

"Great," Telemaco said. "Now we've got to babysit some would be wiseguy."

"He'll probably only be in town a few more days," Williams said.

"How long has he been here so far?"

"I don't know." Williams looked down at the "missive" again. "Looks like he took the plane in three days ago."

"And we're just hearing about it now?" Telemaco said. "Who knows what he's been up to so far?"

"I guess first I'll have to find out what hotel he's in," Williams said.

"Okay, you do that," Telemaco said. "Maybe I can catch up on some paperwork before we have to go out and take a look at him."

"You and paperwork," Williams said, shaking his head. "If you just stayed up to date, you wouldn't have to catch up so often."

"You do your paperwork your way and I'll do mine my way," Telemaco said.

Williams picked up his phone. "I'll check the chain hotels first."

There was no point in going to the French Quarter and just hanging out in Jackson Square, hoping to catch sight of Vincent Napoli. So Sangster decided to wait until Burke had some solid information.

During his days as a hitman, he had traveled extensively. But since setting up house in Algiers Point, he spent many hours and days on his front porch, which he was happy to do. He felt no impatience with doing nothing. Nothing felt good, every day. The only time he interrupted his nothing routine was when Burke or Father Patrick came over to play chess, or when he went out to get something to eat.

Or when something totally unwanted entered his life, reminding him of who he used to be, before he had a soul.

He was drinking coffee when Burke came up the walk, only hours after he'd brought the ex-sheriff his beignet breakfast.

"Got any more of that?"

"In the kitchen."

"I'll get it."

"I was going to say, help yourself," Sangster said.

Burke went inside, came out with an oversized mug of coffee. The mug was huge, one Sangster had found in the Quarter, a souvenir for the tourists. He knew it would suit Burke's appetite for coffee.

"Ah!" Burke said, as he sat. It was either in anticipation of the coffee, or in relief of getting off his octogenarian legs.

"What do you have for me, Burke?" he asked.

"Well," Burke said, "from the looks of your house you could use the loan of Polly to clean—"

"Never mind that."

"Well, sure," Burke said, "fine, far be it from me to criticize how you live. I found your guy."

"That was fast."

"Well, he's in the Marriott on Canal Street."

"Not hiding, is he?"

"Obviously not."

"Well, all right." Sangster stood up. "I might as well go and see him."

"What, now?" Burke raised his coffee mug.

"Finish your coffee," Sangster said. "I have to change."

"Clean up a bit while you're in there," Burke called after him as he went inside. "It looks like you've been burgled."

"Eat me!"

The ferry from Algiers dropped him off on Canal Street. They were able to walk to the hotel from there, and would be able to walk into the French Quarter if the need arose.

When they reached the hotel, Sangster said, "First let's see if he's still registered, and then we'll see if he's in."

"It's after noon," Burke said.

"Meaning?"

"He's probably out sightseeing."

"You think he's here sightseeing?"

"He was in Jackson Square, wasn't he?"

"He was, indeed," Sangster said, and entered the hotel lobby.

SEVEN

Sangster received all the information the desk clerk was allowed to give, that Vincent Napoli had registered at the hotel, had indeed arrived, and was still a guest. The man then directed him to the nearest house phone.

"Do you know if he's presently in his room?" Sangster asked.

"I don't know that, sir," the young clerk said, "but if you call his room you might be able to find out."

"Thank you."

Sangster turned from the desk and walked to where the house phones were. Burke, elsewhere in the lobby, watched him go. He had the one photo they had of Vinny Napoli, and was watching people as they walked through the lobby.

Sangster went to a phone, got the operator and asked for Vincent Napoli's room. The phone ring ten times before he hung up and rejoined Burke.

"There's no answer," he told Burke.

"Either that or he's not answering."

"It rang ten times. I don't think he's there."

Burke smiled. "Then he's sightseeing after all."

"Maybe."

They turned to leave the hotel, but as they did, two men came through the front doors and stopped in front of them. From the surprised looks on their faces,

Sangster knew this was a coincidence.

"Well, well," Detective Telemaco said. "Imagine meeting you here, Stark." He was speaking to Sangster, using the name Sangster went by in New Orleans. Then he looked at Burke. "Hello, Sheriff."

"Detective," Burke said.

"Telemaco," Sangster said. "It's been a while. And, Detective Williams. How…nice."

"What are you boys doin' here?" Williams said.

"Probably the same thing you are," Sangster said.

"And what do you think that is?" Telemaco asked.

"Looking for somebody," Sangster said.

Telemaco turned and exchanged a glance with his younger, black partner.

"But it's probably not the same person," Burke said.

"You feel like tellin' us who?" Williams asked.

"We're workin' a confidential job," Burke said.

Telemaco looked at Sangster and grinned.

"You a private eye now, Stark?"

"He's helpin' me," Burke said. "I just needed some… backup."

"Backup," Telemaco said. "You guys wouldn't be carrying, would you?"

Sangster spread his arms and said, "Search me," hoping that would satisfy the two cops and they wouldn't find Burke's new Glock the older man had tucked into the back of his belt.

"Naw, that's okay," Telemaco said. "Put your arms down." He looked at Williams. "I mean, what are the chances we're here looking for the same guy, right?"

"We'll be on our way, then," Burke said. "Make our next stop."

"Hopefully," Williams said, "we won't run into you there, too."

"Now that," Telemaco said, "would be too much of a coincidence, wouldn't it, Mr. Stark?"

Sangster and Burke nodded, moved past the two detectives and out the front door.

"What do you think that was about?" Williams asked, Telemaco.

"To tell you the God's honest truth, partner," Telemaco said, "after everything that happened last year, I don't really want to know."

As they headed for the front desk, Williams said, "You still haven't told me everythin' that happened last year."

"I know," Telemaco said.

Outside Burke wiped his brow. "What made you think they wouldn't search us?"

"It seemed a chance I had to take," Sangster said. "Besides, I'm not even wearing a jacket, where would I be hiding a gun?"

"I'm wearin' a jacket," Burke reminded him.

"It's more of a shirt," Sangster said, "and not really that heavy."

Burke was wearing a T-shirt and jeans, as Sangster was, but had thrown the "jacket" over it to hide the gun.

"Besides," Sangster went on, "they were wearing jackets, too."

"They're wearin' suits," Burke pointed out.

"And not very expensive ones, either," Sangster said. "Now let's get the hell away from this hotel before they change their minds and come out here looking for us."

The two New Orleans detectives approached the desk and spoke to a female clerk. They asked the same questions Sangster had asked, but since they showed her their badges, they got more answers.

"Yes," she said, "we do have a guest by that name."

"Do you know if he's in his room now?" Telemaco asked.

"I'm sorry, no, I don't," she said.

Her name tag identified her as Kathy.

"You're very pretty, Kathy," he said. "He doesn't flirt with you when he goes in and out?"

She laughed and said, "No, Detective, he doesn't. Are you flirting with me now?"

"I wish I was," Telemaco said, "but I'm way too old for you, I'm afraid. Now we're going to need his room number."

"And I'm afraid," she said, "that I'll have to have the Assistant Manager give you that. And he'll probably want to walk you up there."

"Well, Kathy," Telemaco said, "I don't think that'll be a problem for us. Why don't you call him?"

"Yes, sir," she said. "It'll just be a minute."

"Thank you."

She turned away, then turned back and asked, "Doesn't he talk?" pointing at Williams.

"Only when he wants to," Telemaco said.

* * *

Kathy moved further down to another station and picked up a phone. As she did, the other clerk came over next to her.

"They're asking about the same man?"

"Same as who?" she asked.

"Another man was just here," he said. "He was asking about that same man, Mr. Napoli."

"What did you tell him?"

"Nothing."

"Was he a cop?" she asked.

"No."

"Well, these two are," she said. "They have badges and everything."

"Do you think I should tell them?" he asked.

"Naw," she said, "let Mr. Hedges handle it. I'm calling him now. After all, he's the Assistant Manager."

"Yeah," the male clerk said, "he's always reminding us of that."

EIGHT

"Do you think they'll find out we were askin' about the same guy?" Ken Burke asked, as they walked into the French Quarter.

"Maybe," Sangster said.

"So what will we tell them when they ask why?"

"I don't know. We'll have to deal with that when the time comes."

"And where are we goin' now?"

"Well," Sangster said, "we could go back and just sit in the lobby, wait for him to come back."

"But we'd have to explain what we were doin' there."

"Probably."

"So?"

"The alternative is to go to Jackson Square and see if he's there, again."

"Doin' what?"

Sangster shrugged.

"Watching the dancers, getting his cards read, having lunch. Whatever."

"And if he's not?" Burke waved the answer away. "I know, we'll deal with that when the time comes."

* * *

It had been a while since Sangster had been in the Quarter, which included Jackson Square—and having a Lucky Dog.

"Where to first?" Burke asked.

Sangster pointed to the hot dog vendor.

"Oh, I see," Burke said, "you brought me here to try and kill me."

"One Lucky Dog isn't going to kill you."

"With my digestive system?"

"Well then you can just watch me eat one, old man," Sangster said.

"Why don't we have a real lunch in one of these cafes? You know, sit outside, look at the girls, keep an eye out? You can get a Lucky Dog later, before we head back to Algiers."

"Okay, fine," Sangster said, "you pick one."

Burke chose Muriel's, a favorite of his because it served both Creole and Cajun food.

They didn't sit outside. Sangster thought they'd be too conspicuous. Instead, they sat at a window table, so they could see out, but not everybody could see in, depending on how the light reflected off the glass.

"I love this place," Burke said.

Sangster looked at the Cajun dish Burke was consuming and said, "You were worried about what a Lucky Dog would do to your system? That's hot!"

"And spicy," Burke said, happily. "I love it. It's all about the crawfish and hot chili peppers—"

"Yeah, yeah," Sangster said. "I'll let the doctors know when you collapse." He paid attention to his more edible, less deadly étouffée.

While they ate they stared out the window at the passersby who were enjoying what Jackson Square had to offer.

"You've missed it, haven't you?" Burke asked. "The Quarter?"

"Very much."

"Do you really think anyone else from your old life will come lookin'? It's been a while."

"Only months," Sangster said, "not years. I've been thinking it might be time for me to move on."

"You mean, leave Algiers?"

"I mean leave New Orleans—and Louisiana."

"And go where?"

Sangster shrugged.

"You're gonna leave all this?" Burke said, spreading his arms to encompass not only the food on the table, but the shenanigans that were going on in Jackson Square.

"I know," Sangster said, "it won't be easy, but I'm thinking I better go before somebody else gets hurt."

"Like who?"

"I've let too many people into my life, here."

"Yeah, you have. Me and the priest. You cut the nurse out."

"I had to," Sangster said. "And don't forget Polly and her kids."

"They're not around you all the time."

"Too much for their own good."

"I think you better give it some more thought."

"I will."

* * *

They finished their meal and had coffee before leaving Muriel's.

Burke was watching two pretty girls in short skirts walk by, shaking his head. "It's hell gettin' old."

"Who are you kidding? You get more tail than I do."

"Yeah, but it ain't tail like that."

"Never mind," Sangster said, "Polly gives you all you can handle." Polly was Burke's Creole cleaning woman and his lover. She had two daughters and a son who Sangster had met and helped a few months back, when one daughter went missing.

"You got that right," Burke said, with a big grin. "You're still jealous about that ain'tcha?"

"You bet," Sangster said.

"You shouldn't've let that nurse go."

"Don't start that again, Ken."

"Okay," Burke said, putting his hands up, palms out, "I'm jus' sayin'."

"Let's get out of here," Sangster said. "This has been a waste of time."

They paid their bill and left the restaurant.

"Where to? Back to his hotel?"

"The police might still be there, waiting for him," Sangster said. "Let's just go back home. I'll start again tomorrow, with a new plan."

"Okay, but we've got one more stop to make first."

"We do?"

"You forgot?" Burke asked. "Café du Monde!"

"Oh, right."

Vinny Nap was walking up Canal Street toward his hotel as dusk was falling. He'd eaten in a restaurant that had lots of noise and loud music, and enjoyed every minute of it. He loved the French Quarter. There was nothing like it in Philadelphia. All he had back there was his constant effort to be accepted by the Abbatello family. Maybe he should just stay here.

He was down the street from the hotel when he saw the two men. New Orleans or Philadelphia, he knew cops when he saw them. He turned, went back the way he had come, and turned down Chartres Street, walking toward Common. That would take him behind the hotel. Perhaps he could find a back way in.

As he turned on Common, he felt something interesting press into the small of his back.

"Cops," a man's voice said. "I saw them, too."

Vinny tensed.

"No, don't turn around, Vinny," the man said. "Keep walkin'."

"What's goin' on?" Vinny asked. "How do you know me?"

"What does that matter?" the man asked. "I do."

"So this ain't a robbery?"

"Not hardly."

"It's a hit."

"That's such an old word," the man said. "I prefer to think of this as a solution to a problem."

"I ain't no problem."

"You are to some people."

"And you're the solution?"

"That's what I get paid for."

"What if I pay you more?"

The man laughed. "You haven't got a dime."

"Now look—"

"Over there," the man directed. "That's where the laundry's delivered."

"Somebody'll see us!"

"No they won't," the man said. "There won't be any more deliveries today. I did my research."

"There are cops out front."

"I know," the man said. "We talked about that, already. Don't worry, they won't hear a thing."

"L-look," Vinny said, "you ain't gotta do this—"

"Oh, but I do."

"I ain't just gonna—"

"Go ahead," the man said. "Run. You've got nowhere to go."

Vinny looked around. There was no one around, no one to call out to, just the back of the hotels with closed doors. He could turn and run, but the man was right. Where could he go?

"Did the family send you?" Vinny asked, suddenly calmer.

"Would it help you to know?" the man asked. "Make you feel better?"

"Maybe."

"Well then…" the man said, and then Vinny heard the *phhht* of a silenced pistol and there was nothing else…

NINE

The next morning Sangster took his breakfast—a mug of black coffee and some toast—out to the front porch with him. He sat there, chewing and sipping, thinking how much he'd miss Algiers and the French Quarter if he left, how much he'd miss his house and his neighbor, Burke, who was probably the only friend he'd ever had, aside from the kids from his boyhood.

He was eating the last piece of toast when a car pulled up in front of the house and two men got out. Detectives Telemaco and Williams came up the walk toward him.

"'Morning, gents," Sangster said.

"Good morning, Stark," Telemaco said, coming up the steps. "Got any more of that?"

"Coffee or toast?"

"Coffee will be fine," Telemaco said.

"Have a seat," Sangster said. "I'll get you each a cup."

He went inside to the kitchen, filled two more mugs and then refilled his own. He carried all three out to the porch, a balancing act.

"Thank you," Telemaco said. Williams simply nodded and accepted the cup.

"What brings you by this morning?" Sangster asked. He remained standing. It gave him a slight advantage.

Williams sat forward and looked at his partner. "Don't we need the sheriff?" he asked.

"Probably not," Telemaco said. "But you could go next door and see if he's there, if you want. Maybe even question him there."

Williams stood, raised his mug to Sangster. "You mind? I'll bring it back."

"No problem."

Williams nodded, went down the steps and headed next door.

"So you need to question both of us?" he asked.

"Just to be thorough," Telemaco said. "After all, we did see both of you at the hotel yesterday."

"So this has to do with the hotel?"

"Did you find the man you and the sheriff were lookin' for?" Telemaco asked.

"No," Sangster said, "did you?"

"We did," Telemaco said, "but a little late."

"What's that mean—oh," Sangster said. "That's why you're here."

"Yeah," the detective said, "he was dead. We found him behind the hotel, shot in the back of the head. Once."

"That's usually enough," Sangster said. "But that still doesn't explain what brings you here."

"His name was Vincent Napoli," Telemaco said. "Known in Philadelphia as Vinny Nap. That name mean anythin' to you?"

"No, it doesn't."

"You sure you don't know him?"

"I can honestly say I never met the man."

"What about Sheriff Burke?" the detective asked. "Think he knows him?"

"Same thing," Sangster said. "Never met him. I'm sure that's what he's telling your partner right now."

"Then what were you doin' at that hotel yesterday?"

"I told you," Sangster said. "I was looking for some-one."

"And you're not gonna tell me who?"

"It's not important," Sangster said. "It's got nothing to do with what you're working on."

"That so?"

"Yes, it's so."

Suddenly, Williams appeared, coming up the walk again. He stopped at the steps.

"You get any more out of the sheriff than I got out of this character?" Telemaco asked.

"I doubt it."

Telemaco stood up.

"You came all the way out here for that?" Sangster asked. "And for coffee?"

Telemaco put his mug down on the table next to the chessboard. Williams leaned in and set his empty mug next to it.

"We also have to see someone else out here."

Telemaco started down the steps.

"Who?" Sangster asked.

Telemaco turned and said, "That's not important for you to know."

He and his partner walked to their car, got in and drove away.

Sangster took the mugs and the plate his toast was on into the house, then came back out and walked next door. He knocked on Burke's front door.

"Oh, it's you," Burke said, opening the door quickly. "I thought it was that cop again. Come on in."

"You alone?"

"Yeah, yeah, It's not Polly's day."

They went into Burke's living room, neat and clean because of Polly.

"He ask you about yesterday?" Sangster asked.

"He did."

"Yeah, his partner questioned me. Said they found Vinny Nap shot to death behind the hotel."

"Have a seat," Burke said. "You want somethin'? Coffee?"

"No, I'm good."

They sat.

"You don't think maybe we shoulda told them we were lookin' for him?" Burke asked.

"Yeah, Burke, I think we probably should've, but we didn't."

"Are we gonna?"

"Not until we talk to Father Patrick first," Sangster said.

"And get his okay?"

"Right."

"When do we do that?"

"Actually, you don't have to do it," Sangster said. "I will. I'll go over there now and let him know that Vinny's dead. Maybe he'll give me the okay to talk to the cops, then."

"That should keep you out of trouble with your friend Telemaco."

"He's not my friend."

"Well," Burke said, "you and him have gone through some things."

Sangster stood up.

"I'll let you know what happens," he said. "And don't worry, I'll keep you out of trouble."

"I'm too old to stay out of trouble for very long," Burke said. "You know that."

TEN

Sangster walked over to Father Patrick's church, with the intention of telling him that he didn't have to worry about Vinny Nap, anymore. As he approached the rectory he saw Telemaco and Williams' car in front of it. There was an alley across the street. He decided to wait there until the detectives left.

It took fifteen minutes before the door opened and the two men came out, got in their car and drove off. Sangster left the alley, crossed to the rectory, and knocked on the door.

The door opened quickly and Father Patrick appeared, his mouth opened to say something. He closed it when he saw Sangster standing there.

"Stark!" he said. "I thought it was those two detectives coming back."

"I saw them," Sangster said, "so I waited until they left."

"Come on in."

Sangster entered, watching as Patrick looked out the door before closing it.

"We better go to my room," the priest said.

Sangster nodded and followed. They went into Patrick's room and closed the door.

"What the hell—I mean, what happened?" Patrick asked.

"What do you mean?"

"I mean...Vinny Nap."

"Yeah?"

Patrick leaned in. "They said he's dead. Somebody shot him."

"That's what I was coming to tell you," Sangster said, "but they got here first."

"Did you...uh..."

"Did I what?"

"Well...you know."

"Are you asking me if I killed him?"

"Well..." Patrick lowered his voice. "I did see you kill somebody, um, once."

"Yes, when he was trying to kill me," Sangster said, "and was probably going to kill you next."

"True..."

"I never even saw Vinny Nap," Sangster said. "Burke and I went into the Quarter to his hotel but he wasn't there. We ran into Detectives Telemaco and Williams, who were also looking for him."

"And you didn't tell them you were?"

"No, we told them we were looking for somebody, but we wouldn't tell them who."

"I see."

"So why were they here to see you?"

Patrick sat down on his bed, his shoulders slumped.

"They said they went into his room and found my name there."

"On what?"

"They didn't say. They just wanted to know where I knew him from."

Sangster pulled out the desk chair and sat down.

"What did you tell them?"

Patrick rubbed his face with both hands.

"I couldn't lie to them" he said. "I mean, I'm a fuc—I'm a priest, after all."

"You told them the truth?"

"Well, no…" he said, sheepishly, "I didn't quite do that, either."

"What did you tell them, then?"

"I told them I knew him in another life."

"Did you tell them where?"

"They asked, but I didn't."

"How did they take that?"

"Not well," he said, "but Telemaco is a Catholic."

"What did that buy you?"

"Twenty-four hours."

"To do what?"

"To tell them where I knew Vinny from," Patrick said. "To tell them if I shot him or if I knew who shot him."

"Well, you don't," Sangster said. "Let's get that clear right now."

"Right, right," Patrick said, waving his hand, "I don't know who shot him. But I'm the only one they think knows him in New Orleans. That means I'm a 'person of interest,' accordin' to them."

Sangster took that in.

"I thought they were going to arrest me."

"It's too early in the investigation," Sangster said. "They have no evidence, yet."

"But they're gonna be lookin' for some," Patrick said.

"Yes, they are."

"You gotta help me, Stark."

"Why?" Sangster asked. "Are they going to find any?"

"Well, no...but if they look hard enough they'll find the connection. And if they find that, they'll think they've found a motive. And if they find that..."

"They'll probably arrest you."

"Unless they can find out who really killed him," Patrick said. "Or you can."

"Okay," Sangster said, "I get it."

"Will you help me?"

"Why not?" Sangster said. "I'm sure they think I'm already involved, anyway."

"In killin' him?"

"In looking for him," Sangster said. "That's all Burke and I did."

"Right, right," Patrick said. "So, where do we start?"

"I'm not a fucking cop, Father," Sangster said, "but at least I know somebody who used to be. We'll start there."

ELEVEN

Detectives Telemaco and Williams drove their car off the Algiers Ferry, then pulled over to the side to let others go by.

"Where to now?" Williams asked.

"Lunch, I guess."

"Where?"

"I don't know," Telemaco said. "You choose."

"Lemme think a minute."

They sat there in silence a few minutes.

"We let that priest off pretty easy."

"Not so much," Telemaco said. "He just needs some time to think."

"We do that because you're Catholic?"

Telemaco looked at his partner.

"You think I laid off him because of Catholic guilt?"

Williams shrugged. Telemaco studied the slender black man's profile.

"What are you?" he asked.

"What?"

"Your religion."

"I'm a Baptist."

"Hmm," Telemaco said. "Well, maybe you're right. We'll give him his twenty-four hours, and then we'll bring him in and squeeze him. Okay?"

"Sure," Williams said.

"So," Telemaco said, putting the car in drive, "where to for lunch?"

Burke handed them each a cup of coffee, then took his own and sat on his sofa. Sangster was sitting in an armchair, while Father Patrick paced nervously.

"Let me get this straight," Burke said. "Now you want to investigate this Vincent Napoli's murder?"

"If we don't," Patrick said, "the police are gonna think I did it."

"You're a priest," Burke said.

"So?"

"Doesn't that mean somethin'?"

"Priests have been known to break the law," Sangster said, "and even kill people."

Burke looked at him. "Yeah, I suppose you're right." He looked at Patrick. "But what do you mean *we*?"

"Well," Patrick said, "I wouldn't know where to start, so I asked Stark to help me."

"And?" Burke asked, looking at Sangster.

"And I'm not a cop," Sangster said. "You used to be."

"And so it's we?" the ex-sheriff asked.

"Well," Sangster said, "you could be, like, an advisor."

Burke thought about it, and then shrugged and said, "Yeah, well…"

"Where would we start?" Patrick asked.

"Who would want Napoli dead?" Burke asked.

"I don't know," Patrick said.

"Well, we don't know," Sangster said. "You've got to have some idea, Father. You did know him."

"Only in passin'," Patrick said. "I mean, he was sort of on the outskirts of the Abbatello family."

"So would the Abbatello's want to kill him?" Burke asked.

"Well...he was more of an annoyance to them than anythin'," Patrick said.

"Okay," Sangster said, "so if he saw you here, called and told them about it, what would happen?"

"I don't know," Patrick said. "I suppose they'd send someone."

"To do what?" Burke asked.

"Probably to kill me."

"Okay," Burke said, "so they sent a hitman here to kill you. What if he first kills Napoli?"

"Why?" Patrick asked.

"Well, you said he's an annoyance," Burke said. "Would they want him to know they had you killed?"

"What else would he think was going to happen when he told them where I was?" Patrick asked.

"Still," Burke said, "he'd be a witness."

"So they kill him," Patrick said, "and I'm next."

"Yes," Burke said. He looked at Sangster.

"I was thinking that whoever killed Napoli would probably go back to Philadelphia—maybe has even gone back already. But if their main reason for coming here was to kill you..."

"Then they're still here," Patrick finished.

"If," Burke said, "they haven't given the contract on Patrick to another man."

The three of them fell silent.

Finally, Patrick asked, "So how do we find him before he finds me?"

"Maybe," Sangster said, "we don't."

"That's what I was thinkin'," Burke said.

"Thinkin' what?" Father Patrick asked.

"We don't go looking for him," Sangster said. "We just wait for him to come looking for you."

"Oh," Patrick said, "I don't like the sound of that."

"Well," Sangster said, "we could go to the cops and tell them your whole story."

"I don't even know the whole story." Patrick looked at him. "And I'm not supposed to ask," Burke added.

"No, no," Patrick said, "I can't go to the police. I mean, why would they even believe me that somebody else killed Vinny Nap and wants to kill me? They'd think I was makin' it up to cover my as—to cover myself."

"He has a point," Sangster said.

"So how do you wanna play this?" Burke asked.

"Well, on one hand we need to keep an eye on Father Patrick in case the killer tries for him."

"And on the other hand?"

"I was thinking maybe I could fly to Philadelphia," Sangster said.

"Philly?" Patrick asked. "What for?"

"To ask some questions."

"But you just said we don't go lookin' for them," Burke said. "We wait for them to come for Father Patrick."

"I know I did," Sangster said, "but that means sitting and doing nothing for who knows how long?"

"And?"

"I don't have the patience I once had."

"So I suppose I'm the one who's gonna have to sit here and wait for somebody to kill Father Patrick."

"Not alone, Burke," Sangster said. "You got a friend you can press into service?"

"I know some retired cops," Burke said. "I'll make some calls."

"I'm going to walk Patrick back to church," Sangster said. "I'll stay there with him until you or one of your buddies shows up."

"I can jump on the computer and book you a flight," Burke said. "When do you wanna go?"

"Tomorrow's good," Sangster said. "And book me a hotel at the other end."

"Expensive or cheap?"

"In-between," Sangster said. "Come on, Patrick."

They left Burke's house and headed for the church.

TWELVE

"Stark, I don't know if it's such a good idea for you to go to Philly," Patrick said, as they walked.

"Why?"

"Jimmy Abbatello is dangerous," Patrick said.

"In what way?"

"Whataya mean?"

"People can be dangerous in different ways," Sangster said. "Is he smart, clever—"

"Jimmy's...crazy," Patrick said. "He used to beat Bobby, his son, as well as his wife, Connie."

"And the wife, she stayed with him?"

"She had too," Patrick said. "If she left him, he'd kill her."

"Do you mean, he'd have her killed?"

"Jimmy has people like Vinny Nap killed," Patrick said. "But his wife, he'd kill her himself."

"And you," Sangster said, "you're the kind he has killed?"

"There was a time I thought he'd kill me himself," Patrick admitted, "but I doubt he'd come here to do it, so he'd probably send somebody."

Somebody like Sangster used to be.

* * *

Sangster and Patrick were in the front sitting room of the rectory, talking about Philly and the Abbatello family. They heard a knock on the door.

"I'll get it," Sangster said.

He found Burke standing there with another man.

"Stark, this is Ralph Hayes. He was a deputy under me for a few years, retired just last year."

"Come in," Sangster said.

The two men entered. Hayes was a good twenty years younger than Burke, in his sixties. They shook hands.

"Burke says you need some help."

"Just a babysitting job for a few days," Sangster said.

"Suits me," Hayes said. "I been gettin' pretty bored lately. Retirement ain't really for me."

"Ralph's not a fisherman," Burke said.

"I been takin' odd jobs, so when Burke said you needed some help I figured, why not?"

"I can pay you—"

"Naw, naw," Hayes said, "I'd be doin' this as a favor for the sheriff."

"Okay, then," Sangster said. "I'll introduce you to Father Patrick."

"What's the priest's problem?" Hayes asked.

"Somebody might be trying to kill him," Sangster said. "Also, the police might come looking for him."

"Well, I can't do much about the cops," Hayes said, "but I guess I can keep him alive."

"Do you have a gun?"

"I've got my old service revolver," Hayes said.

"On you?"

Hayes nodded. "I thought I might be startin' this job tonight."

"Good," Sangster said. "Father Patrick's in the sitting room. This way."

Sangster made the introduction between Patrick and Hayes, and then Hayes and Burke made plans for when the ex-sheriff would relieve him. After that Burke and Sangster walked back toward their houses.

"Wanna stop for a beer?" Burke asked.

"Sure, why not?"

They stopped at the Old Point Bar on Patterson Street. There was usually live music, but on this night it was quiet, which suited them.

When they were seated at a table on the street out front with a beer each, Burke said, "I've got a question."

"Shoot."

"You sure you wanna get involved in this?"

"If I don't," Sangster said, "Patrick might end up dead."

"Yeah, he might."

"Then the answer is yes, I want to get involved."

Burke started, "I haven't been made privy to Father Patrick's real problem with the Abbatello family in Philly, but I can make a guess about why a priest is reassigned to another parish."

"Make your guess, Burke."

Burke sipped his beer, then set the mug down on the table gently.

"You know what?" he said. "I don't think I will. I think I know Father Patrick well enough to know it's not what I was thinkin' it might be."

"I think you do, too, Burke," Sangster said. "According to Patrick it was a misunderstanding, and while I'm no fan of the Catholic Church, I believe what he told me."

"Okay, then," Burke said. "I'm with you."

"Let me ask you a question, now."

"Go ahead."

"Are you sure *you* want to get involved in this?"

"I'm sure I got two friends who need help," Burke said. "That's all I should need to know."

THIRTEEN
Philadelphia, PA

Jimmy Abbatello sat back in his chair and picked up the photo of his late son Bobby, which he kept on his desk. It used to be he couldn't look at that photo without breaking down, but he was all cried out. The last tear had fallen a long time ago. Now he just felt sad when he saw it, but he kept it there, anyway.

The door to his office opened; he quickly put down the photo and watched his wife, Connie, enter and close the door behind her. At one time she was the most beautiful woman he'd ever seen—blonde, leggy, face of a model, perfectly made-up. She was only forty now, but since Bobby's death she had just...faded. Her hair had lost its luster, she didn't wear much in the way of cosmetics anymore, and she'd put on weight. Her waist and calves had thickened.

It used to be when he looked at her, he wanted nothing more than to make love to her. But since Bobby's death each time he tried, he was impotent. It made him angry, and he took it out on her, even though she had lost her son as well. So they stopped trying and didn't really talk much anymore.

"There's no need," she said. "I know you sit in here and stare at his picture."

"Connie," he said, "I'm busy. What do you want?"

"What I've wanted for a long time," she said. "I want the man who abused my Bobby. I want him dead."

"I'm still workin' on that, baby."

"So you say," she said. "Why is it takin' so long, Jimmy?"

"Honey, you know we don't have the resources we once had," Jimmy said. "I'm doin' the best I can with what I have."

"Whatever," she said. "I came in to tell you dinner's in ten minutes."

"Yeah, okay."

She turned to leave. The door opened before she reached it.

"Joseph is here," she said.

"I can see that."

"Connie," Joseph said.

She nodded, opened her mouth to say something else, but backed out of the room without saying it.

Joseph Maniscalco walked into the room, wearing a thousand-dollar suit as usual, his dumpy body making it look like it came off the rack.

"Sit, Joseph."

Maniscalco sat across from his boss. The Abbatellos were no longer one of the top Mafia families. In fact, the Mafia was no longer what it once was. The families were scrambling for footholds in both the legit and crime worlds. However, Jimmy Abbatello was after something else entirely. But no matter what, Maniscalco was still loyal to Jimmy—or rather, to Jimmy's father.

"What have you got?" Jimmy asked.

"Vinny Nap is dead."

"So what?" Jimmy asked. "What about Father Patrick?"

"As far as I know," Maniscalco said, "he ain't dead yet."

"What's Frankie waiting for?"

"I don't know, boss," Maniscalco said. "Maybe he just ain't found him, yet."

"What's so hard?" Jimmy asked. "All he has to do is look in a church."

Jimmy saw something on the lapel of Joseph Maniscalco's jacket as the hefty man shrugged. It looked like a piece of pepperoni.

"Maybe there's lots of churches in New Orleans."

"I knew I should've gone there myself," Jimmy said.

"That wouldn't be smart, boss."

"So now you're tellin' me what's smart, Joseph?" Jimmy asked.

"No, no, boss," Maniscalco said, "that ain't what I meant to do. I'm just sayin' it wouldn't be safe for you to go. You still got enemies."

"The other families?" Jimmy asked. "They're all real busy, Joseph."

"I got my ear to the ground, boss," Maniscalco said. "Like a real consigliere is supposed to."

"Don't even use that word no more, Joseph," Jimmy said. "I'm not my father."

"No, you ain't," the other man said, "but I promised your old man I wouldn't let anythin' happen to you, and I'm gonna keep that promise."

Jimmy looked at Bobby's picture. He'd made many promises to his son, promises he *didn't* keep, and some he *couldn't* keep.

"All right, Joseph," Jimmy said. "But I made one last promise to my son, and I'm gonna keep that one. So when Frankie calls and tells you that he's found Patrick, I wanna know right away."

"And then what?"

"And then we're goin' to New Orleans," Jimmy said. "Maybe I'll just kill Father Patrick myself."

FOURTEEN

Sangster flew to Philadelphia the next morning, having had Burke book him coach fare. He dressed down to avoid notice, jeans and a windbreaker. When he arrived at Philadelphia International Airport he rented a car from one of the smaller, discount desks, a nondescript two-door Nissan and drove to the South Philly neighborhood of Packer Park. Specifically, Jimmy Abbatello had a house in Geary Estates, a section of townhomes that had been built about ten years earlier on the grounds formally occupied by Holy Spirit convent. They were three-story estates with parking for two cars, decks and finished basements. According to Father Patrick, the Abbatello family had moved in when the houses first became available. Jimmy considered it a great status symbol.

"They've fallen on hard times in the past ten years," Patrick had said, "but I think they'll still be living there."

The problem with the Abbatellos living in a neighborhood of town homes was that no matter where Sangster parked, somebody was bound to notice and either call the police or a private security firm.

According to Father Patrick, Jimmy Abbatello still had a consigliere left over from his father's days as head of the family. His name was Joseph Maniscalco. If anyone knew Abbatello's plans and schemes, it would be him. Sangster figured his best bet was to ask Maniscalco some questions, and make it worth his while to answer them.

Father Patrick gave him the consigliere's description, figured he couldn't have changed all that much over the years, except maybe gotten fatter.

"He probably comes to the house in the mornin' and leaves in the afternoon," Patrick had said. "And be careful, he's always heeled."

"I'll be careful."

"You might have to kill him," Patrick said. "He's very loyal to the Abbatellos."

"To Jimmy?"

"No," Patrick had said, "to the family."

"I don't intend to kill him," Sangster said, "just ask him some questions. I won't be asking him to betray the family, just Jimmy."

Patrick had nodded and said, "That might work."

It was already past morning by the time Sangster rented his car and drove to Packer Park. He found a place where there were already some parked cars, and left his among them. Then he walked to where the Abbatellos lived. There were a couple of columns at the end of the winding driveway. He decided to wait there for Joseph Maniscalco to come out. If he was lucky, nobody would notice him.

He hadn't brought a gun with him, wouldn't have been able to get on the plane with one. He could have made a call to an old acquaintance in Philly to get one, but in the end, decided he didn't need one. He wasn't planning on shooting anybody, only asking a few questions. Now all he had to do was figure out a way to get

Maniscalco to stop when he drove out.

He folded his arms and leaned against the column to wait.

On this day, Maniscalco stayed around the house until near dinner time, then decided to leave. Jimmy hadn't had anything for him to do, hadn't come out of his office all day. Connie had spent some time in her room, some in her son's room—which she did, a lot— and some in the kitchen.

"Are you stayin' for dinner, Joseph?" she asked him.

"No, Connie, I'm gonna go eat at Alfredo's."

She rubbed her upper arms with her hands, as if she was cold, and said, "I haven't been out to eat in so long."

"You can come, if Jimmy says it's okay."

"If Jimmy says?" she asked, laughing without any humor whatsoever.

"He's still the boss, Con," Maniscalco said.

"Yours maybe, Joseph," she said, "not mine."

She turned and walked back into the bowels of the house. He went out the front door, got into his Cadillac and drove down the driveway.

Sangster heard the car coming down the drive and decided to play it straight. He stepped out into the path of the old Fleetwood.

The car stopped and the driver's side window rolled down.

"Get the hell out of the way!" the driver shouted.

"Joe Maniscalco?" Sangster asked.

The door opened and Maniscalco stepped out. Father Patrick had said the man might have gotten fatter. Sangster didn't know how heavy he had been, but he was pretty wide now.

"That's Joseph," Maniscalco said, "and who wants to know?"

"I'm in the market for a job," Sangster said.

"What kind of job?"

"The kind you hire out rather than do yourself."

"And what kind do you think that is?"

"Some people call it wet work."

Maniscalco narrowed his eyes until they almost disappeared beneath folds of fat.

"You a mechanic?"

"Some people say that, too."

"You got a name?"

Sangster said something he hadn't said out loud in years.

"Sangster."

Maniscalco studied him for a few moments, then said, "You hungry?"

"Starved."

"Get in!"

FIFTEEN

Maniscalco drove Sangster to his rental car, and then Sangster followed him to a restaurant called Alfredo's on 9th Street in the Italian Market. A maître d' made a fuss over Maniscalco and showed him to his "regular" table. An elderly waiter appeared immediately with two glasses of red wine.

"Thanks, Gino," Maniscalco said.

"Woulda you friend like a menu?" the waiter asked.

Maniscalco looked at Sangster, who said, "Why don't you order for both of us?"

"The veal, Gino," Maniscalco said.

"*Bella,*" the waiter said, kissing his fingertips.

The waiter left and Maniscalco picked up his wine glass.

"I know your name," he said to Sangster. "Haven't heard it in a few years, though."

"I keep a low profile."

"Naw," the consigliere said, "you ain't been workin'. Why is that?"

Sangster shrugged and said, "I took some time off."

"You never did any jobs for us, didja?"

"No."

"Any of the five families in New York?"

"One or two," Sangster said. "I spread myself around, though."

"How wide?"

"Anybody with money."

"And now you're ready to get back in the game?"

"That's right."

The waiter came back with a basket of sliced Italian bread and some butter. He also poured olive oil onto a small plate for dipping.

"So you decided to stake out my boss' house?"

"I heard he's been having some trouble locating a certain person."

"And who would that be?"

"A priest?"

Maniscalco took out a cigarette case and lit one up without offering one to Sangster. The ex-hitman took the opportunity to butter a piece of bread.

"What makes you think you could show up out of the blue and get hired, Sangster?"

"I didn't think it'd be that easy. I figured you'd want to check my bona fides, Mr. Maniscalco."

"And you were right. Who's your handler?"

"Nobody at the moment."

"Then who was it before you went…on leave?"

"That won't help, either," Sangster said. "He's dead."

"That's too bad. Got any local contacts?"

"One or two."

"You mind if I check with them?"

"Not at all."

The waiter came back with two steaming plates of veal piccata and pasta.

"But that can wait until after we eat," Maniscalco said, crushing his cigarette out in an ash tray. "Alfredo's makes the best veal piccata in Philly."

"That's something I'm sure you'd know, Mr. Maniscalco."

"You can just call me Joey, Sangster," Maniscalco said, "for now."

"I appreciate that, Joey."

"Unless you don't check out," the man added, "then you're gonna hafta call me somethin' else."

Sangster put a piece of veal into his mouth without asking what that was. Maniscalco was right. It was excellent.

It had come to Sangster in a flash to play the hitman card, and he had gone with it. "Sangster" was the last name he'd gone by while doing the job and he figured Maniscalco would recognize it—as he did.

Over coffee and cannolis, Maniscalco said, "I guess you know things ain't the way they used to be."

"I figure family's family," Sangster said. "There's always something the family needs done."

Maniscalco nodded. "That's a good way to look at it, I guess."

"So I figured you'd know if Mr. Abbatello needed anything...you know...done."

"Jimmy Abbatello runs a legit operation now," Maniscalco said. "He don't have people killed."

"Anymore?"

Maniscalco pointed with a thick forefinger and said, "I never said he did."

"Everybody knows he did."

"I ain't even checked you for a wire, Sangster," Maniscalco said.

"You want to search me?"

"Not here."

"Then where?" Sangster asked.

"I don't know."

"Look," Sangster said, "I'm just looking for work, Joey."

"And you're work is killin' people, right?"

"Right," Sangster said. "Now I wouldn't be saying that if I was wired, would I, Joey?"

"I don't know, Sangster," Joey Maniscalco said. "Would you?"

SIXTEEN

Sangster and Maniscalco left Alfredo's and stopped on the street just in front.

"Thanks for the meal," Sangster said.

"Just bein' friendly," Maniscalco said.

"I didn't know that was part of your job for the Abbatello Family."

"It ain't."

A car pulled up in front of them and two men in suits got out. As they approached, Maniscalco put some distance between himself and Sangster.

The ex-hitman looked at him and said, "I wasn't the one wearing a wire, huh?"

Maniscalco just shrugged.

"Okay, Joey," one of the men said, "you can go now."

"Sorry, Sangster," Joey Maniscalco said, and walked to his Cadillac.

Sangster looked at the two men, who took Philadelphia P.D. badges out of their pockets and showed them to him. The only thing about the two men that was similar was their badges.

"We need you to come with us, Mr. Sangster," the tall one in the cheap suit said.

"My name is Stark," Sangster said.

"You told Joey it was Sangster," the shorter one in the more expensive suit said.

"Did I?"

The two detectives exchanged a glance.

"We need you to come with us...sir," the shorter one said.

"Am I under arrest?"

"No," the tall one said.

"What are your names?" Sangster asked.

"I'm Detective Abel," the shorter man said, "and this is my partner, Detective Griffith. We're with the Philadelphia Police Department's Criminal Intelligence Unit."

"Ah."

"And we need you to come with us," Abel said.

"Where?"

"To our offices," Griffith said.

"What for?"

"Just to answer a few questions."

"I'll need a ride back to my car when we're done," Sangster said. "It's over near Jimmy Abbatello's house."

"Let's see how our Q-and-A session goes before we make any promises," Detective Abel said.

They drove Sangster to their headquarters at 5301 Tacony Street and installed him in an interrogation room. They were the same in every police station he'd ever been in. A table, chairs, and a mirror on the wall.

They let him stew for a half hour, then both men came in and sat across from him.

"How about some water?" Abel asked, setting down a plastic bottle.

"No, thanks."

"Rather have a glass?" Griffith asked.

Sangster smiled. A glass would give them an even better set of his prints than the bottle would. "No, thanks. I'm good." He kept his hands clasped in his lap, didn't even touch the surface of the desk.

The two detectives exchanged a glance. It seemed to Sangster they had realized they weren't going to get his prints. They must have been surprised to find that he didn't carry a wallet or a billfold, just cash, and the driver's license he had in the name "Richard Stark" was not laminated.

"All right," Abel said, sitting back. It seemed like he was going to take the lead. "What are you doing in Philly?"

"A favor for a friend."

"What friend?"

Sangster didn't answer.

"Is your name Sangster or Stark?"

"It's Stark."

"Why'd you tell Joey it was Sangster?"

"I thought that would get his attention."

"You know who Sangster is?"

"I know the name."

"Well, he hasn't been seen or heard from in a few years, and then suddenly you show up and use his name."

"Like I said," Sangster answered. "I knew the name, thought it would attract some attention. Looks like I was right. Although, I'm kind of surprised to find out that Joey Maniscalco was wired by the Philly P.D. What do you think Jimmy Abbatello would say if he knew?"

"Who says Joey was wired?"

"So you two just happened to pull up in front of Alfredo's when you did?" Sangster asked.

"Even detectives get hungry, Mr. Stark," Abel said.

"What am I doing here?"

"Like we said," Abel replied, "we just have a few questions for you."

"Such as?"

"Why did you tell Joey your name was Sangster?"

"I didn't."

"But—" Griffith started, but a look from his partner stopped him. They couldn't say *But we have you on tape saying just that* because that would be admitting they had Joey Maniscalco wired. And it was Sangster's guess that the wire was not legal.

"All right, never mind that," Abel said. "I don't suppose you'd voluntarily give us your fingerprints?"

"I'm afraid not," Sangster said. "But you can make me give them. All you have to do is arrest me."

"Yeah," Griffith said, "we could do that."

"On what charge?"

"We can come up with something," Abel said, "but why do I have the feelin' that you don't care about that? Your fingerprints wouldn't even be in the system, would they?"

Sangster didn't answer.

"This is a smart man, partner," Abel said. "When he doesn't want to answer, he just keeps quiet. That way he doesn't lie."

Sangster remained silent and waited.

"Where are you staying, Mr. Stark?"

"Holiday Inn Express on North Christopher Columbus."

"And how long will you be there?"

"I don't know," Sangster said. "That depends on how long it takes me to do this favor I have to do for a friend."

"And that favor wouldn't have anything to do with killin' somebody, would it?" Abel asked.

"No," Sangster said.

"Now, that wouldn't be your first lie, would it, Mr. Sangster?" Abel asked.

"My name's Stark."

"Oh, right," Abel said. "That wouldn't be a lie, would it, Mr. Stark?"

"No, Detective, it wouldn't," Sangster said. "Would you like me to state it more plainly for you?"

"Please do."

"I have no intention of killing anyone while I'm in Philadelphia."

Abel looked at his partner. "Well, that makes me feel better, Griffith. Does it make you feel better?"

"Not a bit, Abel," Griffith said. "Not one bit."

SEVENTEEN

The detectives allowed Sangster to leave the building, but would not give him a ride back to his car in Packer Park. He was lucky to catch a cab right out front. When he got to his car he sat behind the wheel and went over the day's events.

Joey Maniscalco worked for Jimmy Abbatello and was wearing a wire for the cops. The question was, did Abbatello know about the wire? Were they using the wire to feed the cops bad intel? Did the cops really think Maniscalco would flip on the Abbatello family? Or did they have something on him, something so heavy that he really was flipping on Jimmy Abbatello?

The mistake he'd made was in using the name Sangster again. It had been years, and the idea had come to him in such a flash he should have discarded it. Instead he said the name and the cops had heard it. Only they couldn't admit they'd heard it without admitting they'd planted an illegal wire.

His best move would be to head right back to New Orleans, except he hadn't learned a thing from his trip to Philly. But the cops knew where he was staying, and he didn't know if Maniscalco had told Jimmy Abbatello about him.

Maybe that was something he should find out.

He started the car, drove it up to the gate, stopped

there. Nobody would be able to get in or out as long as his car was there.

He waited…

It only took Joey Maniscalco an hour to drive down to the gate and open it. But first he asked, "Are you sure about this?"

"No," Sangster said.

"Are you really Sangster?"

"Who told you that?" Sangster asked. "My name is Stark."

"Yeah, okay," Maniscalco said. "I coulda buzzed you in from the house, but I had to make sure. Follow me up."

Sangster followed Maniscalco's Caddy with his rental car, and pulled to a stop in front of the house.

"Come on," Maniscalco said, getting out of his car. "Jimmy's waitin'."

"What'd you tell him?"

"Whatever you told me."

"Lead the way, then."

They went into the house, which had a large entryway with a chandelier. It was supposed to impress people.

There was also a staircase with a faded woman coming down, a woman who had been pretty once. Could have still been, if she'd cared enough.

"Who's this, Joey?" she asked.

"This is Mister Stark, Connie."

"Hello, Mister Stark." Sangster could tell she'd had a few drinks. "Why are you here?"

"To see your husband, Mrs. Abbatello."

"Ah," she said, "you're another one of those, huh?"

"Another one of what, ma'am?"

Before she could answer, Maniscalco said, "Connie."

Connie looked at Sangster, put her forefinger to her lips and walked away into the bowels of the house.

"This way," the consigliere said.

Sangster followed Maniscalco down a hallway to an office, wondering if the man and his wire were going to remain while he talked to Jimmy Abbatello.

"Jimmy," Maniscalco said, as they entered a large office, "this is...Stark."

"Stark, huh?" the man behind the huge desk said. He was about the woman's age, but with a little more vitality. The death of his son had not made him fade the way it had her. But it had an effect on him. Sangster could see it in the man's eyes. The sadness.

"That's what he says."

"Mr. Abbatello," Sangster said.

"I understand Joey bought you dinner, and you came back here and blocked my driveway."

"I did."

"What for?"

"I wanted to be invited inside," Sangster said, "to talk."

"So talk," Jimmy Abbatello said. "What's on your mind?"

Sangster made a point of looking at Maniscalco, who was standing in the doorway.

"Joey," Abbatello said, "go find somethin' to do"

Maniscalco frowned, but withdrew from the room.

"And close the door!"

The door closed.

"Have a seat, Mr. Stark," Abbatello said. "I ain't

gonna offer you a drink, 'cause I get the feelin' this ain't a social visit."

Sangster sat. He wondered if Abbatello had banished Maniscalco from the room because he knew the consigliere was wired.

"What's that all about?" Abbatello asked.

Sangster made another spur-of-the-moment decision.

"Father Patrick."

Abbatello sat up straight, as if he'd been shocked by an electric prod.

"What?"

"The priest you've been trying to find for...how many years is it?"

Abbatello sat forward and scowled at Sangster.

"What do you know about him?" he demanded. "Do you know where he is?"

"What I know about him is he doesn't want to be killed."

"Did he send you to beg for his life?"

"Oh, no," Sangster said, "he doesn't know I'm here."

"Joey said he thought you were lookin' for work," Abbatello said. "Do you wanna kill the priest? Is that it?"

"If I did," Sangster said, "would you call off your other killers?"

Now Abbatello sat back.

"I don't employ killers, Mr. Stark," he said. "I'm afraid you might be believing some wild things you've heard about me."

"You mean like you being head of a Philadelphia Mafia family?" Sangster asked.

"Yeah," Abbatello said, "like that. Ain't no Mafia anymore. Everybody knows that."

"But your father, he was a Mafia Don, right?"

"My old man was head of the Teamsters in Philly for years," Abbatello said. "Everybody knows that."

"Everybody, huh?"

"Look," Abbatello said, "do you know anything about the priest or not?"

"Not where he is," Sangster said, "but I could find him."

"How?"

"That's my business."

"And then what?"

"Do what you want."

Abbatello frowned.

"How much?"

"The going rate," Sangster said, "plus fifty percent."

"You're fifty percent better than anyone else?"

"More than that," Sangster said, "but this is our first negotiation."

"Money up front?"

Sangster shook his head. "That's up to you. I'm satisfied with being paid when the job's done."

"And what do I have to do?"

"Just call off anyone else you've sent out," Sangster said. "I don't want anyone getting in my way."

"You don't like competition?"

"I hate it!"

Abbatello was staring at something on his desk. It took a few moments for Sangster to realize it was a framed photo of his son.

"Mr. Abbatello?"

"Why should I have faith in you?"

"Why shouldn't you?" Sangster asked. "How long have you been looking for this...priest?"

"A long time," Abbatello said.

"Then what do you have to lose?"

"I normally wouldn't do this without references."

"Talk to Joey."

"What does Joey know?"

"Maybe there's something he hasn't told you…yet."

Abbatello studied Sangster for a few moments, then stood up, walked to the door and opened it.

"Joey!"

Sangster heard the big man running up the carpeted hallway.

"Yeah, boss?"

"Get in here."

"Yeah, boss?" Maniscalco asked, entering the room obediently.

Sangster stood before they got started and said, "I'll wait outside."

He left, closing the door behind him.

EIGHTEEN

It became very obvious that Jimmy Abbatello's office was soundproof. All Sangster could hear from the hallway were muffled tones. The outcome was going to depend on Maniscalco's wire. Did he have it on? Did Jimmy Abbatello know about it?

Abruptly, the door opened and Sangster heard Jimmy shout, "Get out!"

Maniscalco came out, wearing the hangdog look of a kicked canine. He glanced at Sangster, and then kept going.

"Stark!" Abbatello shouted.

As Sangster entered the room he saw a change in Jimmy Abbatello. It was subtle, but suddenly the man looked like the head of a Mafia family.

"Close the fuckin' door," he said.

Sangster obeyed.

"This room is swept every day for bugs," Abbatello told Sangster. "That means that whatever you and me say right now is between you and me. You got that?"

"I got it."

"Is it Stark or Sangster?"

Sangster hesitated.

"If you're worried about Joey's wire," Jimmy said, "don't be. There are no wires present in this room."

Sangster studied Jimmy Abbatello, and decided he would tell the truth.

"It's Sangster." Coming clean was for the benefit of Father Patrick. Maybe Sangster could convince Abbatello to recall his killers.

Abbatello say back in his chair and said, "Goddamn. I thought you were dead."

"Not quite."

"So where you been?"

"Here and there."

"You know what?"

"No, what."

"I changed my mind," Jimmy Abbatello said. "I am gonna offer you a drink, after all."

When they both had a glass of bourbon, Sangster sat again, but more comfortably this time. He believed Abbatello that there were no wires in the room.

"How long have you known your consigliere is wearing a wire?" he asked.

"Ever since he told me," Abbatello said, "the day they put it on him."

"You been feeding them bad info?"

"More like no info," Abbatello said. "As far as the cops know, I'm just a businessman."

"But they still think they're going to get something out of Joey."

"That's why he gave them you," Abbatello said. "To keep them satisfied that he was on their payroll. Tell me, how'd you get them to let you go?"

"They don't have anything on a man named Stark."

"What about fingerprints?"

"They didn't arrest me or print me," Sangster said. "And even if they did, my prints aren't in the system."

"That's smart," Abbatello said. "How'd you manage that?"

"By never getting caught."

"How many men you killed?"

"I never kept count."

"That's gotta be a lie," Abbatello said. "Man like you's gotta count."

"The only numbers that ever mattered to me was what I was getting paid."

"All right, then," Abbatello said, "let's talk about what you're gonna get paid to kill that priest."

"First," Sangster said, "let's talk about you calling off the rest of your dogs."

"Dog," Abbatello said. "Just one. He's supposed to be the best. His name's Frankie Trigger. Ever heard of him?"

"No," Sangster said. "Is that really his name?"

"Frank Trigliotti," Abbatello said, "but he's kind of a throwback to the old days, calls himself 'Frankie Trigger.'"

"Well," Sangster said, "I never heard of him."

"He came along during the past three years," Abbatello said, "probably just while you've been gone. Supposedly, he's never missed."

"He get the priest?"

"Not yet."

"Then maybe he's missed his target this time."

"Well," Abbatello said, "last I heard from him, he knew what city the priest was in."

"How did he find that out?"

"Well," Abbatello said, "to tell you the truth, we got

a tip and sent him there to check it out."

"And where would that be?"

Abbatello hesitated, then said, "New Orleans."

Sangster drank down his bourbon and set the empty glass on the desk.

"I think you should call him off," he said.

"And send you?"

"That's right."

"Well," Abbatello said, "you've been out of circulation for a while, Sang—"

"Call me Stark."

"Okay," Abbatello said, "Stark…what if you ain't got what it takes no more?"

"I've got what it takes."

Abbatello thought a moment, turning his glass in circles as he did so.

"Tell you what," he said, finally. "Why don't we make this a little contest between you and Frankie? Find out who really is the best."

This wasn't going the way Sangster had planned. He'd been hoping Abbatello would call his man off, and then he'd have time to figure something out with Father Patrick.

"A contest?"

"Yeah," Abbatello said, "you go to New Orleans, and let's see who gets the priest first, you or Frankie." He spread his arms out. "Winner take all. How about that?"

Sangster just shrugged. "That sounds like as good a way as any to settle it."

NINETEEN

The man who called himself "Frankie Trigger" wasn't used to making mistakes.

He had killed Vinny Nap too soon. But it wasn't his fault. When he'd corner Vinny behind the hotel, his intention was to get him to tell where the priest was. Instead, Vinny panicked, started to run, to yell. Frankie had no choice but to end him.

The priest was in New Orleans. The killer knew that much. So all he had to do now was check every church in town.

Frankie did a search on his tablet and came up with a directory of forty-four Roman Catholic churches in New Orleans. He was going to have to check them one by one. But since Vinny Nap said he saw the priest in Jackson Square, Frankie Trigger started his search with the churches nearest to that location.

He started with St. Louis Cathedral, the oldest continuously active cathedral in the country. While it was a definite stop for tourists in New Orleans, it was not a tourist attraction, but an active place of worship.

It was beautiful outside, breathtaking on the inside, but Frankie was not religious in any way and had no interest in architecture. He was only interested in priests.

Over a two-day period he checked St. Louis Cathedral, Our Lady of Guadalupe, St. Augustine, St.

Patrick's, St. Joseph's, Holy Name, St. Theresa, St. Mary's Assumption and Christian Unity.

Frankie Trigger was a patient man, but he wasn't happy with the food in New Orleans. He hadn't been able to find a decent Italian restaurant, and so far he hadn't had one meal he'd enjoyed. The only thing he came close to liking was the coffee and beignets at Café du Monde.

He was sitting there at a table, watching the tourist girls walk by when the burner he was using for business rang.

"Yeah?"

"Frank?" It was Joey Maniscalco's voice.

"It's my phone, ain't it?"

"Hold on for Mr. Abbatello."

"Sure, Joey."

After a few seconds, Jimmy Abbatello came on the line.

"You find the priest yet?" he asked.

"There's more than forty Catholic churches in New Orleans," Frankie said. "I'm checkin' them. I'll find him."

"You killed Vinny Nap too soon, Frankie."

"I told you, Mr. Abbatello," Frankie said. "He didn't give me no choice."

"Yeah, well, you're not givin' me any."

"What's that mean?"

"I'm sendin' somebody else to New Orleans."

"What for?"

"One of you will get the job done," Abbatello went on. "And one of you will get paid."

Frankie put his coffee down and sat up straight.

"Wait, what? This isn't a competition, Jimmy."

"It is now, Frank."

"Who are you sending?" Frankie demanded. "One of your idiots? Not Joey!"

"Sangster."

Frankie hesitated a few seconds, then said, "What?" in total disbelief.

"You heard me."

"Sangster's dead."

"Naw," Jimmy Abbatello said, "he took some time off. Now he's back, and he's comin' to New Orleans."

"This is a joke, right?"

"No joke, Frank."

After a moment Frankie asked, "There's nobody listenin' to this call, is there?"

"No ears, no wires, Frank," Abbatello said. "Or I wouldn't be sayin' your name, right? Or his."

"Sangster."

"Right."

"He's alive."

"Right."

"And comin' here?"

"Now you're gettin' it."

"Is he comin' to see me?"

"No, Frank," Abbatello said, "he's comin' to kill Father Patrick."

TWENTY

Sangster took a shower as soon as he got home. He wanted to wash all of Philly off.

He came out of the shower, pulled on a T-shirt and jeans, grabbed a Blackened Voodoo from the fridge and took it out to the front porch. The chess pieces were in their box, which was sitting on top of the board. He sat at the table in his customary chair, but left the pieces where they were.

The trip to Philly did not go in any way as he would have expected. He actually had no plan when he went, so he couldn't say it hadn't gone as planned. But the way it had turned out was a bigger surprise to him than it would be to Burke or Father Patrick.

He knew only one thing he hadn't known before the trip. The killer looking for Father Patrick—who had already killed Vinny Nap—was named Frank Trigliotti. And, apparently, he was a throwback to the days of "Sammy the Bull" Gravano and Abe "Tommy Karate" Pitera. He apparently was now what Sangster used to be—the best killer in the business.

Sangster had no idea who "Frankie Trigger" was. If the man had made his bones in the past three years only, then he had literally come out of nowhere. Unless he was a man Sangster knew who had simply changed his name.

He had half his beer left. He decided to finish it at his leisure before going to St. Mary's to inform Father Patrick that he, Sangster, had apparently accepted a contract to kill him.

When he knocked on the door of the rectory, Burke was the one who opened it.

"You're back," the ex-sheriff said. They shook hands. "Good to see you."

Sangster entered and Burke closed the door after checking the street.

"Everything okay?"

"Huh? Oh, yeah, I just like to be careful. Come on, we're just sittin' down to eat. Hungry?"

"Yeah, I am."

As they entered the dining room, Burke said, "I'll ask Mrs. Cox to set another place."

"Stark!" Father Patrick said from the table. "Glad you're back and in one piece. Have a seat."

Sangster sat on the priest's right. There was already a place set for Burke on his left.

"Wine?" Patrick asked, picking up a decanter of red.

"It's not sacramental, is it?"

"Nope," Patrick said, "just a nice merlot."

"Then I'll have some."

Patrick stood, went to a breakfront, got another glass, filled it and handed it to Sangster.

"How'd the trip go?" he asked, reseating himself.

"It was…interesting."

Burke came in at that point with the makings of a place setting—plate, utensils, napkin.

"She told me to do it myself," he said, brandishing

them with a smile. He set everything in front of Sangster, then sat across from him.

Mrs. Cox came in and covered the table with food. There was more than enough for the three of them.

"What about you?" Burke asked her.

"I usually eat in the kitchen," she said, and backed out of the room. Sangster eyed the chicken and scallops with creole rice, waiting his turn to help himself.

"So?" Patrick asked. "How did it go? Did you see Jimmy?"

"I saw him," Sangster said. "Talked to him."

"You actually spoke with him?"

"I did."

"Where?"

"His house."

Patrick dropped his fork onto his plate in surprise.

"You went to his house?"

"I did," Sangster said. "First to talk with Joey Maniscalco."

"How did that go?"

"He bought me lunch at Alfredo's."

Patrick laughed, a loud bark. "He what? That's his favorite place."

"I know. He told me."

"He never takes anybody there," Patrick said. "At least, he didn't used to."

"Well, he took me."

"And?"

"And then he got me in to see Jimmy." Sangster skipped the part about the police and the wire.

"Just like that?" Patrick asked, picking up his fork again.

"Well, there was a little more to it," Sangster said,

"but the point is, I got in to see him."

"And? Did you get me off the hook?"

"No," Sangster said, "he still pretty much wants you dead."

"So what did the two of you talk about?"

"Well," Sangster said, "I found out who killed Vinny Nap, and who's going to try to kill you."

"That's somethin'," Burke said.

"Who is it?"

"He goes by the name Frankie Trigger. Supposed to be the best hitman in the business."

"Jesus."

Burke frowned.

"I never heard of him," the ex-sheriff said.

"Apparently," Sangster said to Burke, "he's come along in the past three or four years. Since you retired."

Burke's look said to Sangster, "Since you retired, too!"

"And what happened?" Patrick asked.

"Well," Sangster said, "to put it bluntly, he hired me to kill you."

TWENTY-ONE

"He—you—what?"

"I got him to hire me to kill you," Sangster said. "It was the only way I could keep him from sending more men after you."

"What about the one who killed Vinny Nap?" Burke asked. "Frankie Trigger?"

"He's still here."

"Here?" Patrick asked.

"In town," Sangster said.

"But where?" Burke said.

"My best guess? He's looking for Patrick at Catholic churches in New Orleans."

"Then he'll find his way here, eventually," Burke said.

"Probably," Sangster said. "We'll need to take Patrick somewhere else."

"Like where?" Burke asked.

"I think my house would be fine."

"But doesn't Jimmy know who you are?" Burke asked.

Sangster frowned. Jimmy thought he was "Sangster," but knew him as "Stark." The old sheriff was probably right.

"How about your house, then?"

"That might not be such a good idea."

"Why not?" Sangster asked.

"Somebody's been watchin' your house," the ex-lawman said, "so, by the same token, they've kinda been watchin' mine."

"Who's watching?" Sangster asked. "Cops?"

"Could be," Burke said.

"Probably Telemaco," Sangster said. "I'll bet he's put a man on me."

"Frankie?" Patrick asked.

"I doubt he knows much about me," Sangster said. "I doubt Jimmy will even tell him my name."

"What *will* Jimmy tell him?" the priest asked.

"That it's a competition, now," Sangster said. "Whoever kills you gets the money."

"Any idea how much money?" Patrick asked.

"Does it matter?"

Patrick shrugged. "I'm just curious what my life is worth, these days."

"Jimmy didn't tell me," Sangster said. "He just said it was top dollar."

"So if not your house and not my house, where can we put him?" Burke asked.

"Not in a *Catholic* church," Sangster said, "that's for sure."

"Ah," Burke said, "there're a lot of other houses of worship in New Orleans."

"Including," Sangster said, "some very interesting local ones."

"Local?" Patrick asked.

"He means Voodoo houses of worship," Burke said.

"B-but I'm a Catholic priest," Patrick said. "What would I do there?"

"We'll figure something out," Sangster said.

* * *

After they finished eating, Burke walked Sangster to the door.

"Stay with him tonight, Burke," Sangster said. "I'll take some time to figure out someplace to take him."

"And what about whoever's watchin' your house?"

"I'm thinking maybe I'll have a talk with them tonight," Sangster said. "But maybe I'll give Telemaco a call first, see what he has to say."

"This late?" Burke asked, raising his bushy eyebrows. "You got his home number?"

"I've got his cell number," Sangster said.

"Let me know what happens, then," Burke said. "And be careful walkin' home."

"I'll be fine," Sangster said. "I'm hard to find in the dark when I want to be."

Sangster left the rectory. Burke closed and locked the door behind him.

Sangster walked toward his house, but before he reached it he decided to go through Burke's backyard and see if he could spot whoever was watching.

He crossed the yard to Burke's back porch, but didn't see anybody. Then he moved up along the side of the house, until he was next to the front porch. That was when he saw the glow of a cigarette tip across the street from his house. There were a couple of abandoned buildings there. He figured the smoker was standing in the doorway of one of them.

He returned to Burke's back steps, sat down and dialed Detective Telemaco's number on his cell phone. It rang half a dozen time before it was answered.

"This better be good," Telemaco said.

"Don't tell me you're asleep," Sangster said.

"Let's just say I'm in bed," the detective said. "Whataya want, Stark?"

Sangster heard a woman in the background say, "Who is it, honey? We were kinda busy."

"It's work, doll," Telemaco said.

"Girlfriend?" Sangster asked.

"I wish," Telemaco said. "Wife. Whataya want?"

"I was out of town, Detective, just got back tonight and noticed somebody's watching my house. He's not doing a very good job of staying hidden. You need to hire better help."

"What?" Telemaco sounded genuinely puzzled. "What the hell are you talkin' about?"

"The man watching my house," Sangster said. "Isn't he one of yours?"

"Why would I have somebody watchin' your house, Mr. Stark?" Telemaco asked.

"Yeah," Sangster said, "I agree. Why would you?" He broke the connection and put the burner phone into his pocket before the detective could say another word. Let him go back to doing whatever he was doing to his wife.

Sangster returned to the front of Burke's house and looked across the street until he spotted the cigarette glow again and pinpointed it.

If this wasn't one of Telemaco's men, then maybe he should find out who it was.

TWENTY-TWO

The watcher was becoming impatient.

He'd been there for two days, without being told exactly why. He lit another cigarette, cupping it in his hand to hide the glow. He'd done a lot of jobs in his time, jobs he didn't understand, but this was the first time he'd been watching an empty house for this long.

He drew on the cigarette, but before he could exhale the smoke, an arm wound around his neck from behind and tightened. He couldn't breathe.

"I'm going to loosen my hold so you can exhale the smoke in your lungs," a voice said in his ear. "If you do anything more than that I will break your neck. Do you understand?"

The watcher did his best to nod. It was very short but effective. The pressure around his chest lessened and he exhaled the smoke.

"Wha—" he started, but the pressure was renewed.

"I didn't tell you to talk, did I?"

The watcher tried to shake his head.

"Now, just stand still while I search you."

He felt a second hand pat him down, remove the .38 from his belt holster, then take his wallet from his pants. It was too dark in the doorway for the man to read his ID, though.

"Okay," the man said into his ear, "I'm going to let

you go, but I've got your gun. We're going to walk to the house across the street. If you try to run or yell, I'll shoot you in the spine. Got it?"

"I—I got it," the man said. "L-look, I'm just—"

"Shut up and walk!" Sangster said. "We'll talk when we're in the house."

Sangster turned on the lights in the house, pushed the man ahead of him into the living room and pointed the gun at him.

"Have a seat," he said. "Don't move or speak until I tell you."

The man sat on the sofa. He was a twitchy man in his forties, very short and thin. He was wearing a windbreaker that had seen better days, sweat stains all over it—some of them fresh.

Sangster opened the guy's wallet with one hand while holding the gun with the other. He had no intention of killing the man, but the fellow didn't know that.

"Henry Dickensly, private investigator," Sangster read from the ID in the wallet. He then tossed the wallet aside and turned his attention to the man on the sofa.

"What are you doing here?"

"I was hired to watch this house."

"And me?"

"I don't know who you are," Dickensly said, "so no, just the house. I was watching for somebody to come home, though."

"And then what were you supposed to do?"

"Make a call."

"To your client?"

"That's right."

"Who is it?"

"I don't know," Dickensly said. "I was hired over the phone, paid by messenger."

"When?"

"Just two days ago."

Did whoever hired the P.I. know that Sangster had gone to Philly, and wanted to know when he got back?

"So on the phone," Sangster asked, "was it a man or a woman?"

"I'm not sure."

"Did they use some kind of scrambler?"

"Nothin' that fancy," Dickensly said, "but it was pretty muffled. It could have been a woman with a deep voice or a man with a high voice."

"Do you often take jobs that way?"

"Mister," Dickensly said. "Look at me. I take jobs any way I can get 'em."

"Maybe you should change jobs. I could see your cigarette from across the street, clear as day."

"Yeah, well that's what happens when you smoke three packs a day. Can't go very long without lighting one up."

"And why this?" Sangster said, indicating the gun in his hand.

"I take that everywhere I go," Dickensly said. "I've taken too many beatin's not to."

"If you're lying to me, you're going to take another one."

"Look, dude," Dickensly said, "I'm just doin' what I was paid to do."

"Where's your cell phone?"

Dickensly took a cheap looking flip phone from his pocket.

"Toss it here."

He tossed it and Sangster caught it with one hand. He opened it and went to the contacts.

"This last number," he said. "Is that the one you're supposed to call?"

"That's right."

Sangster looked at the number. Because of the nature of cell phones, the first three digits—usually the area code—didn't tell him anything about where the owner of the phone was located. The area code usually reflected where the phone had been purchased and activated.

"Okay," he said, "let's call."

"Wha—" Dickensly broke off when Sangster tossed him back his phone. The man juggled it, but managed not to drop it.

"Make the call."

"What am I supposed to say?"

"What did they want you to say?"

"They wanted me to call when I saw somebody go into the house and turn the lights on."

"Make the call," Sangster said. "Tell them I'm here."

"And then what?"

"You tell me."

"I don't know!" Dickensly insisted. "I'm supposed to make the call and then go home."

"Well," Sangster said, "that's what you're going to do. Make the call."

Dickensly was obviously not sure whether or not Sangster was telling the truth. Still not sure if he was going to walk out of the house under his own steam. He flipped open the phone and made the call.

TWENTY-THREE

Sangster sat in the living room with the lights on. He still had Dickensly's gun, because he didn't have his own in the house. They weren't part of his everyday life anymore.

He didn't know what the intention was here. Was someone being dispatched to the house to kill him? Or talk to him? Or just watch him? Or maybe to follow him? But for any of those eventualities, the question was the same—why?

The only way the hired killer, Frankie Trigger, could know about him was if Jimmy Abbatello had called and told him. He would also have had to tell him that a man named "Stark" had come to Philly claiming to be a man named "Sangster." But neither "Stark" nor "Sangster" was on any of Sangster's bills. The "Stark" name was only on a phony driver's license he had for emergencies. There was no way Trigger could know that he lived out here in Algiers Point.

This had to be something else, something unconnected to the hitman trying to find and kill Father Patrick.

While sitting there waiting for his visitor, Sangster tried to come up with a good place to store Patrick until he could find Frankie. He had to figure out a way to get the priest off of Jimmy Abbatello's personal hit list.

He was still mulling that over when he heard someone come up on the front deck. Then there was a knock at the door.

Sangster got up with the .38 in his hand. He wouldn't use it unless it was a life-threatening situation. Once there, he looked out the glass carefully. A long-haired figure stood there. The figure knocked again, and Sangster turned the knob.

"Well, hello," the woman said. "I assume you're Mr. Stark?"

"Who the hell are you?" Sangster asked.

Instead of answering, she looked down at his right hand, which was hanging at his side, holding the .38.

"Oh, you won't be needing that, Mr. Stark," she assured him. "I'm only here to talk."

"For that you hired a man to watch my house for two days?"

"What else could I do?" she asked. "I've been having trouble nailing you down. Do you mind if I come in?"

"If you don't mind being searched first."

"Why would I mind?" she asked, then added with a slight frown, "Strip search?"

"Let me see your purse."

"Don't have one," she said. "Just this jacket I'm wearing."

"Wallet?"

"Didn't think I'd need one tonight."

"Hands up, then."

"My pleasure."

She raised her hands and he ran his palms over her body, finding it tight and without an inch of fat. He traced her long legs, checked her boots, then backed away from her.

"Satisfied?"

"Come on in," he said. "Tell me what this is all about."

"Thank you."

She walked past him, trailing behind her a scent that was more soap than perfume. He also noticed she was almost as tall as he was.

He followed her into the living room, the gun almost forgotten in his hand. If this woman had intentions of killing him, she was going to have to do it with her bare hands. Or with assistance from outside.

"This is very…comfortable," she said, turning to face him. "I don't know what I expected, but this…this is you."

"Me?" he asked. "Do you have any idea who I am?"

She smiled at him and said, "I know exactly who you are. And I know everything that went on in Vegas earlier this year."

A few people knew pieces of went on in Vegas, but Sangster thought he was the only one who knew everything.

"You gonna offer a girl a drink?"

"I've got beer."

"That's good enough. Local?"

"Yes, in a bottle."

"Sounds good."

He gestured with the gun—just to bring it into play again—and said, "The kitchen's that way."

"Shall I lead the way?" she asked, and did so without waiting for an answer.

They went into the kitchen, where the woman opened the refrigerator and took out two bottles of Blackened Voodoo. She popped the tops off both of them and held one out to Sangster. He accepted with his empty hand.

"Let's go back to the living room," he said, "and you can introduce yourself."

They returned to the living room where the woman said, "Let's get comfortable, Mr. Stark. Or should I call you Sangster?"

TWENTY-FOUR

"Roxy," she said. "Well, Roxanne, but you can call me Roxy."

"Roxy what?"

"We'll get to that later," she said. "After..."

She was sitting on the sofa, he was in the chair across from her. He still had the gun, but was holding it in his lap, not actually pointing it at her. With the other hand he tipped the beer bottle, drinking from it. She did the same, a solid drink, not a dainty sip. He liked that.

"After what?"

"After we talk."

"Don't make me ask, Roxy."

Roxy leaned forward, put her bottle on the coffee table, removed her jacket and set it aside. Underneath she was wearing a sleeveless blouse that gaped to show some solid cleavage.

"A girl likes to be asked, Sangster," she said. "Or should I call you Stark?"

"Neither one is my real name," he said. "Why don't you just tell me why the fuck you had a man watching my house, and what the fuck you want, Roxy?"

"Well," she said, "I know that Sangster is the last name you were using when you were...shall we say, in the business?"

"And what makes you think that?"

"I don't think it," she said. "I know it."

"Okay," he said, "we're not getting anywhere, Roxy. I'm going to give you five more minutes and then I'm tossing you out—"

"Maybe it would help," she said, cutting him off, playing with a lock of her long, red hair, "if I told you my last name?"

"I don't know," he said. "Would that help?"

She picked up the bottle and took another long drink. "I think maybe it would."

"Okay, then," he said, "what's your last name?"

"My name is Roxanne Primble," she told him.

He didn't react, except to drink.

"Primble, Sangster."

He still didn't respond.

"You killed my father in Vegas?" she said. "He used to run you?"

Sangster set aside his beer bottle. "I need something stronger. How about you?"

"Sure, sure. Whatever you've got."

He nodded, put the gun down on the table between them, and walked to a sideboard where he kept the liquor. He got two highball glasses and poured several fingers of bourbon into each. As he carried them back to the chair, he saw that the gun was still where he had put it. He set her glass down next to the .38.

"Thank you, Sangster." It was a test, to see if he'd still argue the point about the name. He didn't. He sat down across from her and took a healthy swig from the drink. The bourbon burned its way down as he closed his eyes.

"I didn't know Primble had a daughter," he said,

finally, opening his eyes. "What are you, twenty-five, maybe six?"

"You're sweet," she said, picking up her drink. "I'm thirty-one."

His actual guess would have been thirty-two.

"My father kept me away from his business associates," she said. "I went to school in Europe, made my bones there."

"Made your bones?"

She drank some of the bourbon and set the glass down.

"I killed people," she said. "For money. You're familiar with the concept."

"And he didn't know?"

"Not a clue," she said.

"And your mother?"

"She knew," she said. "She's the one who told me what he did, after they got divorced."

"She knew?"

Roxy nodded.

"And then?"

"And then she died."

"Did he have her killed?"

"You know," she said, "I can't answer that. Her death looked like a heart attack, but who knows?"

"How often did you see your father?"

"Almost never," she said. "I lived with my mother until I was twelve, and then they sent me to Europe. He came to see me once or twice. I hardly remember him."

"So how do you know about me, then?"

"I told you, he tried to keep me away from his business associates, but I met some of them anyway," she said. "And they talked. Some of it was about you."

"Talk?"

"Pillow talk, if you like. I did what I had to do to find out what I needed to know."

"Which was what?"

"Well, who I was," she said. "Where I came from. What I was born to do."

"And you think you found that out?"

"Damn straight I do," she said. "I was born to kill people, like you were."

He finished his drink, went back to the sideboard and poured himself another, then turned to look at her. The gun was still where he'd left it. If she was there to kill him, she'd had plenty of opportunities.

"You're right. I may have been born to it," he said, "but I've changed."

"Come on," she said, "you killed him in Vegas earlier this year."

"I don't do it for profit anymore," he said. "And not at all, if I can help it."

"Ah," she said, "I see. Got religion?"

"Something like that."

She studied him for a moment, then set her glass down on the table.

"You're serious, aren't you?"

"Yes."

Before she could say anything else there was a knock at the door.

"Expecting anyone else?" she asked.

"No," he said, "you?"

TWENTY-FIVE

Sangster walked to the door and peered out into the darkness. He was surprised who he saw there.

"Detective Telemaco," he said, as he opened the door.

"What the hell do you mean calling my phone, interrupting me, and then hangin' up like that?" Telemaco demanded. "What's goin' on?"

"Calm down, come in and I'll try to explain," Sangster said. He needed some time to think of a story, so inviting the detective in seemed like a good idea.

As they walked to the living room, Sangster said, "I hope your wife wasn't too upset with me. I'm sorry I interrupted—"

"Forget that part," Telemaco said. "It's gettin' to be a real chore just to fuck my ol' lady."

"Has she gained that much weight?" Roxy asked.

Telemaco did a double take, then took a long look at Roxy, who had stood up as the detective and Sangster entered the room. He observed her long legs that were encased in her tight jeans.

"Naw, it ain't that," he said. "I just got a lot of stress in my life right now. It's messin' with the old equipment."

"That's too bad," Roxy said.

Telemaco looked at Sangster and raised his eyebrows.

"Detective Telemaco," Sangster said, "meet Roxy."

"Roxy?"

Sangster left it at that.

"Detective?" Roxy asked.

"N.O.P.D.," Telemaco said.

Roxy took a couple of steps forward and they shook hands. The detective was impressed by her firm grip. The detective looked at the beer bottles and highball glasses on the table. Sangster noticed that the gun was no longer there. He didn't have enough information about Roxy Primble—if that was her name—to determine whether or not she was telling the truth or if she was crazy enough to take a shot at a cop. He was determined to watch her closely.

"Nobody else?" Telemaco asked. "I'm not interrupting a party, am I?"

"No," Sangster said.

"We started with beer," Roxy said, "and then my host decided to try and get me drunker quicker with bourbon. Would you like a drink?"

"No, thanks," Telemaco said.

"Oh, I'm sorry," she said. "Are you on duty?"

"Actually, I'm not," he said, "but I better not go back to my wife with liquor on my breath." He looked at Sangster. "I was just wanting to make sure everything was all right. Mr. Stark, here, rarely if ever calls me when I'm off duty, late at night."

"Everything's fine," Sangster said. "I shouldn't have called you. I overreacted to a situation."

"That doesn't sound like you."

"Well...we all make mistakes."

Telemaco looked at Roxy, still standing, and then back at Sangster.

"We'll have to talk," he said. "Later."

"Sure."

"Roxy," Telemaco said, "nice to meet you."

"You, too, Detective."

Sangster walked him back to the door.

"Not too much later," Telemaco said, before leaving.

"Right," Sangster said.

After the detective was gone, Sangster went back into the living room and found Roxy standing there with the .38 in her hand. They stared at each other for a few seconds. Then she leaned over and put the gun back down on the table, and picked up her drink.

"I didn't think you'd want this out in the open, no matter who was at the door."

"Good thinking," he said.

She held her glass out. "Refill?"

TWENTY-SIX

He poured her another drink and handed the glass back.

"Is that cop a friend of yours?" she asked.

"I don't think friend is the right word."

"Acquaintance, then?"

"That's as good a word as any."

"Does he know the real you?"

"He knows the man I am now," Sangster told her.

"What about Vegas?" she asked. "Does he know about what went on in Vegas?"

"Never mind Vegas."

She laughed shortly. "He does! He knows about it!"

Sangster didn't bother telling her that Telemaco had been *in* Vegas.

"Does he know your real name?"

"Nobody knows my real name."

"Right, right," she said, nodding. "Did my father?"

"No!"

"Okay, okay," she said, "I'll stop asking about your name—or names. You got anything to eat in the house? I'm starving."

"Roxy," he said, "I'm not going to feed you. You just tell me what you're doing here."

"Sure, right," she said, "right, okay. I need you, Sangster."

"For what?"

"You were the best killer who ever worked for my father," she said. "So I need you to train me."

"What?"

"Yeah," she said. "I've done some killing, but none of it with the…class that you showed over the years."

"How do you know—" he started, then stopped and said, "Never mind. What made you think I'd train you?"

"Well," she said, "if you don't, I'll tell everybody you know who you really are and what you really do."

"I don't know that many people," he said. "I keep pretty much to myself."

"So no friends? No family? No," she said, "that's right, you have no family. But friends? Come on. What about that detective?"

"I told you," Sangster said. "He's not a friend."

"So you live here alone, and you spend all your time alone."

"Yes."

"And that chess set on the porch?" she asked. "You play alone?"

"That's right."

"Chess is a two-man game."

"I study chess problems," he said.

"Yeah," she said, "maybe. Look, if you want, I'll pay you."

"You don't have enough money."

"You sure of that?" she asked. "I've got all my father's money. He left it to me."

Sangster wondered what else her father might have left her—like files?

"Come on," he said, reaching out for her hand.

"Where?"

"You said you were hungry."

TWENTY-SEVEN

He took her to the Old Point Bar on Patterson. She ordered a burger and fries, washed it down with an Abita. He had a bottle of the local beer, as well.

"How much do you know about your father and his business?" Sangster asked.

"Everything," she said. "I know everythin'."

"How could that be?"

"He left me his money," she said, "his property…he left me everything."

"So that includes…what? Files? Computers?"

Roxy shrugged and said, "Everything," and popped a French fry into her mouth.

Sangster sat back in his chair.

"I'm still not sure I believe you," he said.

"What do you want?" she asked. "A birth certificate?"

He leaned forward.

"If you have everything your father had," he said, "including his files, then you should be able to give me somebody's name who could vouch for you."

"Like who?"

"I don't know," he said. "That's going to be up to you."

She bit into her burger and set it down, staring at

him. He watched her chew, swallow, and then lick her lips.

"So this is a test."

"You could look at it that way."

He reached out and grabbed a fry from her plate. It was a gesture of familiarity that surprised him. What was it about her that made him leave the gun home, and then steal a French fry?

"Help yourself," she said.

"Thanks." He took another, this time dipping it in the ketchup on her plate.

When she'd finished eating, they ordered two more Abitas.

"Okay," she said, "I'll come up with a name for you. Then you can check me out."

"Good."

"Then what do we do after you've satisfied yourself that I'm Primble's daughter?"

"I don't know," he said. "I've kind of got something going on, so…"

"What's going on?" she asked. "Maybe I can help."

He stared at her a moment.

"Maybe you can," he said, "but let's see what name you give me."

"Okay."

As they walked back to the house through the dark street, Roxy asked, "So why'd you quit?"

"It's complicated."

"How complicated could it be?"

"I just didn't want to do it anymore," he said.

"So does that mean you wouldn't have pulled the

trigger on me in your house if I'd tried something?"

"I wouldn't have wanted to," he said, "but I wouldn't have let you kill me."

"Ah…so it's a matter of…morals? Because I didn't think you had any of those."

Sangster preferred not to talk about his discovery that he had a soul, so he said, "That's as good a way to put it as any."

When they reentered his house, Roxy said, "How about a night cap?"

"Just one, then you have to go." He got her the drink and handed it to her.

"None for you?"

"I'm done for the day."

"So you quit killing for money and drinking?"

"I quit a lot of things."

"Sex?" she asked raising her eyebrows?"

"No," he said, "I still have sex. Are you proposition-ing me?"

"I was just asking." She drained her glass and put it down. "You got a paper and pen?"

He walked to a small desk, grabbed what she needed and handed it to her. She sat for as long as it took to write something down on the paper, then stood and handed it to him.

"Check me out," she said. "I'll be in touch."

"Where are you staying?"

"Don't worry about it."

"What about a cell—"

"Why would you want to call me?" she asked. "What if I leave here and you never hear from me again? Wouldn't you prefer that?"

"Actually," he said, "I would. And I'd also like to never see your P.I. again."

"Don't worry," she said. "He's fired. Thanks for dinner. Good night, Mr. Sangster."

"Good night, Miss Primble."

He didn't walk her to the door, just watched her leave from where he stood in the living room. Once she was gone he looked at the name written on the slip of paper: MICKEY GREY.

Mickey lived in Brooklyn, Illinois, had an office in the back of a strip club. If you needed information and you could pay for it, you called Mickey.

Sangster took out his cell phone, dialed Mickey's number.

"Hey, Mickey," Sangster said, when the man came on the other end, "it's me."

"Sangster? Hey, man," Mickey said. "It's been a while. What can I do for you?"

"Roxy Primble," Sangster said. "Tell me everything you know about her."

TWENTY-EIGHT

Roxy was, indeed, Primble's daughter.

At least, that's what Mickey Grey said. Mickey also reinforced what Abbatello had said about Frankie Trigger. He was, indeed, generally considered to be Sangster's heir apparent.

"He's good, Sangster," Mickey said. "You better be at your best if you're gonna deal with him."

Sangster had known Mickey for a long time. If he trusted anyone in his life, it was Mickey. But Mickey Grey believed in money more than anything else. Would he have taken money from Roxy to lie to Sangster?

He made a pot of coffee and carried a full mug out to the front porch. There were no cigarette tips glowing in the dark across the street. He believed Roxy when she said she fired the private detective. He just hoped she wasn't intending to hire another one.

Okay, he had to forget about Roxy and her long legs and think about Father Patrick's problem. Now that he had been "hired" to kill the priest, he had to find the hitman Frankie Trigger and convince him not to kill Patrick. But how to do that he had no idea. If Trigger was anything like Sangster used to be, you'd have to kill him to give up a contract. And Sangster didn't have any intention of killing him. So he'd have to come up with a plan, all the while putting Jimmy Abbatello off. And during all that, hope that Trigger wouldn't find Father Patrick first.

Part one of the plan had to be to put Father Patrick someplace safe. Someplace not on the list of Catholic Churches in New Orleans.

Sangster presented himself at the rectory the next morning about ten. Burke answered the door.

"Breakfast?" Burke asked. "We just finished, but I'm sure Mrs. Cox can fix something."

"No, I ate," Sangster said. "I thought we'd just get going. I think I've got just the spot picked out."

"Where?"

"Well, it's not set, yet," Sangster said. "We'll have to ask. And I thought we'd take Father Patrick along with us."

"Do you need me as backup?" Burke asked. "Should I bring my rod?"

"That's up to you," Sangster said, "but I could probably use an extra pair of eyes."

"I was just havin' some fun," Burke said. "You know I'll come along."

When they reached the sitting room, Sangster saw that it was empty.

"Where's is Father Patrick?" he asked.

"He went to his room after breakfast. Want me to get him?"

"I can do that," Sangster said. "Are you sure you don't want to take a break?"

"Hey," Burke said, "I'm showered and fed. I'm ready."

"Okay, then. I'll go get Patrick and we'll get started."

"I'm gonna have another cup of coffee while I wait."

Burke went to the kitchen while Sangster went upstairs to knock on Patrick's door.

"Come!" Patrick said.

Sangster opened the door and went inside. Patrick was sitting at a small, neat desk against the wall, his back to the door. He looked over his shoulder at Sangster.

"Hey, it's you. Good mornin'."

"'Morning," Sangster said. "I'll need you to pack a few things, Patrick. Maybe enough for a week. There's no telling how long it will take me to locate Frankie."

Patrick was apparently finished with whatever he'd been doing. He stood up and faced Sangster.

"Am I going into hidin'?"

"You are."

"What about my parishioners?"

"They'll have to do without you for a little while," Sangster said. "If you stay here you'll be taking a chance that they might have to do without you forever."

"Well, don't sugarcoat it for me," Patrick said, sarcastically. "I'll pack a bag and meet you downstairs. Where are we goin'?"

"You'll see," Sangster said.

Burke was working on his coffee, sitting at the dining room table.

"Want one?" he asked, raising his mug.

"Sure."

"You'll have to pour it yourself. Mrs. Cox is out."

Sangster went into the kitchen, poured a mugful of coffee and carried it out to the dining room.

"What do you have in mind for hidin' our priest friend?" Burke asked.

"Fella I met earlier this year might hide him," Sangster said, "but I'll have to ask."

"And where's this fella?"

"Down by the lake."

"Wait a minute," Burke said, "you mean Allemand, the guy Polly sent you to see when I was in the hospital?"

"That's him."

"He took you out to the bayou."

"That's right."

"You're gonna hide Father Patrick on the bayou?"

"It's an idea."

"Jesus," Burke said, "won't nobody look for a Catholic priest out there."

"That's the general idea."

TWENTY-NINE

Lew Allemand and his boat were right where Sangster had left them months ago, at the end of a pier on Lake Pontchartrain.

"I should thank that man for helpin' you out," Burke said. "It saved my life."

"I thanked him," Sangster said. "Believe me, he doesn't like it. He's kind of a quiet guy."

"So what do we do?" Patrick asked.

"Wait here while I talk to him. I'll wave you over if things go okay."

Sangster started walking down the long pier, which would lead to Lew Allemand and his sad-looking boat.

Sangster was surprised that, like the last time he was there, Allemand was concentrating on tying flies. He wondered why the man never seemed to spend time cleaning his small wooden fishing boat.

Just as Sangster was about to reach the boat, Allemand turned and looked over his shoulder at him.

"Whatchoo back fore, man? You ain't goin' back out to St. John's Bayou, is you?"

"Not this time, Lewis. But I do have another favor to ask of you."

"Polly got trouble again, Stark?"

It had been Burke's housekeeper and woman, Polly, who had sent Sangster to Allemand. Burke had been in the hospital, the apparent victim of a Voodoo curse that was holding him in a coma. Sangster had needed a ride out to St. John's Bayou to find a proper houngan to remove the curse—if there actually was one. In either case, after his trip out to the bayou, Burke woke up.

"No," Sangster said, "It's not Polly who has a problem this time. It's a friend of mine."

"Oh yeah? Whodat?" He put down the fly he was working on and gave Sangster his attention. The black man's forearms were powerful, with ropey, bunched muscles. His skin was smooth and creamy, and not as chalky as some older Creole men. Sangster knew for a fact he was seventy years old, but he could have gone ten years either way.

"See those two men at the end of the pier? One of them is a Catholic priest, Father Patrick."

"What kind of trouble does a Cat'olic priest have?"

"Somebody's trying to kill him."

"Who try ta kill him?"

"A professional hitman."

"Holy shit," Lewis said. "What he do dat somebody hire a hitman?"

"It's a misunderstanding," Sangster said.

"You should try to help him wit' dis misunderstanin', you."

"I am trying," Sangster said. "That's where the favor comes in."

Lewis frowned. "What dis favor?"

"I need a place to keep him where he'll be safe," Sangster said.

"Until when?"

"Until I work this out, fix it so no one is trying to kill him."

"And how long dat take?"

"I don't know," Sangster said. "I'm hoping no more than a week."

Allemand leaned over to look at the two men.

"Who dat other man?"

"That's Burke."

"Sheriff Burke?" Lewis asked. "Polly's Burke?"

"That's right," Sangster said. "He's helping me."

"Polly say Burke a good guy," Lewis said. "And you a good guy, right?"

"Well...in this instance, I suppose that's true."

"So you want me to take him out to the bayou?"

"I don't think we need to go quite that far, Lewis," Sangster said. "I just thought you might know some-place, um, non-Catholic to take him."

"I know lots of non-Cat'lic places, me," Lewis said. "Maybe I should meet your friend?"

"Yeah, maybe you should."

THIRTY

When Sangster waved, both Burke and Father Patrick walked down the pier.

"Father Patrick, meet Lewis Allemand, a good friend of mine," Sangster said.

"Mr. Allemand," Patrick said. Lewis stood up and the two men shook hands.

"Father Patrick," Lewis said. "I don't know nuttin' about Cat'lic priests. Only holy people I knows is houngans and mambos."

"And I don't know much about them," Patrick admitted, "but everybody's entitled to their own religious beliefs."

"Mr. Stark say somebody tryin' ta kill you. You know who and why?"

Patrick looked at Sangster before he said, "I might."

"Okay," Lewis said, waving a big hand, "I don't need know why, me. You care where I takes you?"

Before Patrick could reply Sangster said, "As long as it's somewhere safe."

"Oh, it be safe," Lewis said. "I guarantee, me." He looked at the retired sheriff. "You Burke?"

"I am."

"Polly say you a good man, you."

"Well, Polly's a good woman," Burke said.

Lewis looked at Sangster.

"Okay," he said, "I take your friend—but I don't tell you where I take him."

"Wait," Burke said, "that's not—"

"Burke," Sangster said. "If we don't know where he is, nobody will." He looked at Patrick. "What do you think?"

Patrick shrugged and said, "I guess it sounds okay."

They all looked at Lewis.

"I don't say nothin', me," he said. "You want me to keep him safe, I keep him safe."

"That's the whole point," Sangster said.

Burke shrugged and said, "It's your call."

"It's Patrick's call," Sangster restated.

Patrick passed one hand over his face and said, "Okay look, if this is what it'll take to get Jimmy off my back."

"With you someplace safe, I'll be able to give all my attention to doing that," Sangster assured him.

"Then let's do it," Patrick said. "I'll need to get my bag from your car."

"I'll walk with you," Burke said.

They headed for the car.

Sangster turned to Allemand. "Thank you, Lewis. I'd like to pay you—"

"I'm doin' a favor, me," Lewis said. "I don't take no money."

"How about for gas?"

Lewis turned and looked at his boat, then back at Sangster.

"For gas, I take money."

They dickered for a moment and Sangster finally

gave the man less money than he'd intended.

As the footsteps began to approach behind him, Sangster looked at the boat again. It was made of weathered wood which looked like it could use a paint job. The pilot house had clean windows and a long antenna indicating a radio on board. There was a hatch leading below, which made Sangster curious.

"Tell me, Lewis," Sangster said, "how many does your boat sleep below?"

Lewis smiled, his teeth just slightly yellowed.

"I don't share my bunk, me," he said. "Your friend won't be on my boat."

"That reminds me," Sangster said. He turned to face Patrick, who was carrying a mid-sized suitcase and pulled two burner cell phones from his pocket, handing one to the priest. "Take down this number, Patrick. You're the only one who'll have it, so when this phone rings I'll know it's you."

"Sounds cool," Patrick said. "If we're anywhere near a cell tower, right?" He wrote the number on a scrap of paper and stuck it in the pocket of his black pants.

"And lose the collar," Sangster said. "We don't want anything to make you stand out. And first chance you get, buy a T-shirt."

"I got T-shirts," Lewis said. "I give him one."

Patrick looked at the grease-and-sweat covered T-shirt Lewis was wearing and told Sangster, "Don't worry, I'll buy a few."

THIRTY-ONE

"Where to?" Burke asked. He sat behind the wheel of his 2012 Chevy Malibu. He'd gotten it cheap at a public auction. Being an ex-sheriff had its perks and he'd gotten a tip to be there early.

"Good question," Sangster said. "Let's get a beer at the Napoleon House and figure it out."

The Napoleon was on the corner of Chartres and St. Charles Street in the French Quarter. It was a two-hundred-year-old landmark that served the finest New Orleans cuisine. Sangster wanted to sit at the bar, but Burke suggested a table in the courtyard. Sangster ordered a bottle of Crescent City beer, but Burke went for a Pimm's Cup and a muffuletta sandwich. Both were house specialties of Chef Chris Montero, who had been brought in after the 2015 change of ownership from the family who had owned the place for a hundred years.

"Sure you don't wanna eat somethin'?" Burke asked.

"I only intended for us to have a drink and talk things over," Sangster said.

"Yeah, but look where we are," Burke said. "I couldn't resist."

When the waiter brought their drinks, Sangster gave the Pimm's Cup a look. Made of gin, fresh lemonade, 7-Up and a slice of cucumber, it had never been something that appealed to him.

"I don't know how you can drink that."

"It's refreshin'," Burke said.

Sangster drank his beer and scowled.

"So you don't like the Pimm's Cup," Burke said. "You don't have to scowl about it."

"It's not that," Sangster said. "It's what I've got myself into."

"With Father Patrick?"

"What am I supposed to do if I find this guy Trigger?" Sangster asked. "I'm not going to kill him. Talk him out of his contract? Fat chance."

"You must have had some kind of a plan while you were in Philly."

"Jesus," Sangster said. "In Philly things just went sideways. I played it by ear, and I think I went fucking deaf. Now I'm stuck in this situation and I have no idea what to do next."

"Seems pretty simple to me."

"Well good," Sangster said, "enlighten me."

"You have to find Frankie Trigger," Burke said. "The rest will come to you."

Sangster frowned, drained his beer and waved at the waiter for another.

"Is there somethin' else buggin' you?" Burke asked.

"Yeah, there is," Sangster said.

"I figured."

The waiter came with Burke's muffuletta and Sangster's second beer. After he left the ex-hitman told Burke about Roxy Primble.

"Do you think she's on the level?" Burke asked.

"I checked up on her," Sangster said. "She seems to be."

"Ah, but is the person you checked with on the level?"

"That's a good question," Sangster said, "but for now I've got to trust what he told me."

"Okay," Burke said, "so she's Primble's daughter. Now what happens?"

Burke still wasn't sure what Sangster used to do for a living—at least, not officially. And while he knew that Sangster and Primble had a past association, he didn't know exactly what it was.

"What does she want?"

"Something I don't want to give her."

"Ah," Burke said. "So in all this stuff she inherited from her father, is there somethin' that might cause you some...trouble?"

Sangster thought about that for a moment, then said, "There might be."

"So is she blackmailin' you?"

"No," Sangster said, then added, "not yet, anyway."

Burke sipped from his Pimm's Cup, then pointed to the plate where the other half of his muffuletta sat. He still held much of the other half in his hand.

"Want that half?" he asked.

Sangster eyed it, then said, "Sure, why not?"

THIRTY-TWO

"Catholic churches," Sangster said.

"What?"

"Catholic churches," he said again.

They had moved to the bar after finishing the sandwich, and Burke had joined Sangster in drinking beer—except that he chose Abita while Sangster stayed with Blackened Voodoo, which he drank at home.

"What about them?" Burke asked.

"Frankie boy is going to be searching for Father Patrick in churches," Sangster said. "All we have to do is pick up his trail."

"And how do we do that? We don't know where he started lookin'," Burke said. "If we knew what hotel he was stayin' in, we could guess, but—"

"Tell me something," Sangster said, "if you were looking for a Catholic priest in New Orleans, where is the first place you would go to ask questions?"

Burke thought a moment, then said, "I guess I'd start with the biggest church in town."

"The Cathedral," Sangster said.

Burke nodded.

"Drink up, then," Sangster said, "and we'll take a walk to Jackson Square."

* * *

While the great Cathedral fronted Jackson Square its address was actually 615 Pere Antoine Alley. It was so old that it was literally always undergoing some sort of restoration work. Sangster and Burke had to skirt scaffolding to get in the door.

On the other side of the Cathedral was Pirate's Alley. The last time Burke was there he ended up unconscious and in the hospital.

They entered on the Pere Antoine side.

"What are we lookin' for?" Burke asked.

"Somebody to talk to."

Burke looked around. There were a few people sitting in pews, others walking around studying artwork on the walls: the icons and windows.

"Who?"

"Someone in authority."

"Ah. A priest?"

"Preferably."

Burke pointed toward the front of the Cathedral. Up on the altar a priest was talking with some people, and pointing.

"Okay," Sangster said, "he'll do."

"…Cathedral is not only haunted by Pere Antoine and Pere Dagobert, but by the ghost of Madame LeLaurie," the priest was saying.

"Excuse me," Sangster said.

The priest turned away from his audience of about a dozen people and looked at Sangster. He was a young, red-haired man with a lot of freckles and green eyes. At the moment, his face reflected annoyance.

"Sir? I'm in the midst of a tour—"

"I only need a minute, Father," Sangster said.

"Are you old enough to be Father?" Burke asked.

"I am a Seminarian," the priest said. "My name is Father Sean. Can I help you?"

"I need to talk to someone in authority," Sangster said.

"Authority?"

"Someone who can tell me where to find a priest."

"I can tell you what priests you can find here, if that's helpful."

"It's not. I need someone who can tell me where to find a certain priest."

"Ah," Father Sean said, "that would be the Diocese."

"Diocese?"

"They're in charge of assigning priests to parishes."

"Okay then," Sangster said, "Where do I find the Diocese?"

"Seven-eight-eight-seven Walmsley Avenue. Can I go back to my tour now, please?"

"Sure, Father," Sangster said.

He and Burke turned to walk away, but then he turned back.

"One more thing, Father?"

"Yes?" Father Sean said, impatiently.

"Has there been another man here recently, in the past few days, asking the same kinds of questions? Maybe you told him about the Diocese?"

"I don't know," the priest said. "I'm not always here. If your friend found his way to the Diocese, they'll most likely be able to tell you there."

"Okay, Father. Thanks."

Sangster and Burke left the Cathedral, stopping outside in Pere Antoine Alley.

"Shouldn't we try to find another priest?" Burke asked. "Maybe an adult? One who might be able to answer questions?"

"No, I think Father Sean had it right," Sangster said.

"If Frankie got to the Diocese, they'll be able to tell us."

They walked to Burke's car and got in.

"Hey," the ex-sheriff said, "do you think Trigger's even his real name?"

"As much as Sangster is mine," Sangster said. "Start the car, Burke."

THIRTY-THREE

Walmsley Avenue was in the Marlyville-Fontainebleau area, which meant the Diocese of the Catholic Church in New Orleans was situated amongst four hundred thousand dollar homes.

They didn't need to see a cardinal or a bishop or even a priest. Mrs. Eileen Devine was the Archdiocese secretary and supposedly knew everything there was to know about all the parishes in Louisiana.

They were allowed into her office, found the middle-aged, faded, no-nonsense looking woman seated behind a small, cherry wood desk.

"I'm not sure I understand why you're here," she said, after they introduced themselves. "Who are you again? I mean, aside from your names?"

Sangster looked at Burke, who got the message. He took out his Sheriff's Department ID he carried, the one that said RETIRED across it.

"Former Sheriff Burke, ma'am," he said. "Mr. Stark is my colleague."

"Former Sheriff, you said?"

"That's right."

"And what can I do for you, Former Sheriff?"

"We're wonderin' if a man has been here recently lookin' for Father Patrick…from Holy Name of St. Mary's in Algiers?" Burke had suddenly realized that he didn't know Patrick's last name—or even if "Patrick" was his real name or his "priest" name.

Mrs. Devine leaned back in her chair and stared at them, her face expressionless, but her eyes working. She seemed to be trying to make up her mind about something.

"Do we need something else?" Sangster asked. "Like his last name?"

"No, no," she said, waving her hand. "I can certainly look up who is presently assigned to St. Mary's."

"And did you?" Burke asked.

She removed her wire-framed bifocals, then passed a hand across from forehead. She looked distressed.

"I've talked to the police about this."

"About what?" Burke asked.

"There was a man here asking me the same question," she said.

"When?" Sangster asked.

"Yesterday, in fact."

"Did he identify himself?" Burke asked.

"No," she said, "he simply threatened me."

"How?" Sangster asked.

"With a gun."

Burke looked surprised.

"A man walked into the Diocese with a gun?"

"He didn't have it in his hand until we were alone," she said. "He asked me about Father Patrick, just like you did, only he didn't know what church he'd been assigned."

"And you told him?" Burke asked.

"I told him I couldn't give him that information. That it was against the rules."

"Is that true?" Sangster asked.

She looked at Sangster. "No. I just didn't like his attitude."

"So then what?" Burke asked. "He took out his gun?"

"No," she said, "he just pulled aside his jacket to show me he had one. And I was wondering why he was wearing a windbreaker in this heat. Well, he showed me." She stared at Burke's windbreaker, which he was using to cover his own gun. Sangster was wearing a T-shirt and jeans, so she switched her gaze to him.

"You felt threatened," Sangster said.

"I certainly did."

"So you told him where Father Patrick was?"

She put her glasses back on and glared at both men.

"No," she said. "I don't like feeling threatened."

"So what did you tell him?" Sangster asked.

"I made a show of looking at my computer," she said, inclining her head toward the flat screen monitor on her desk, "and then told him we didn't have a Father Patrick."

"Did he believe you?"

"Not at first. But I think I convinced him."

"And he left?" Sangster asked.

"I finally decided he wouldn't shoot me. Not in here. Too many other offices, other people."

"What if he had tried to walk you outside?" Sangster asked.

"I would've screamed."

Sangster and Burke exchanged a glance.

"You're a very impressive lady, Mrs. Devine," Sangster said.

"You fellas want to tell me what this is about?"

"Wait," Sangster said, "you said you talked to the police?"

"I called nine-one-one after he left," she said. "Two policeman came and took a report."

"Have you talked to any detectives?"

"No," she said. "Only the two policemen."

"There will probably be some detectives here to see you," Burke said.

"And I'll talk to them," she said, "like I'm talking to you, Sheriff."

"Ex-sheriff."

"Just why are you fellas looking for Father Patrick?"

"We're not looking for Patrick," Sangster said. "We're trying to find the man with the gun."

"Why would you want to find a man with a gun?"

"To keep him from killing Patrick," Sangster said.

For the first time Mrs. Devine looked surprised. "Oh, my."

THIRTY-FOUR

Back in the car Burke said, "That's a tough lady."

"Yes, she is," Sangster said.

"You think she was tellin' the truth?" Burke asked. "About not tellin' Frankie Trigger where Patrick was assigned?"

"I don't know," Sangster said. "The lady was a hard read. But I think maybe we ought to drive out to Algiers and have a look see."

"Gotcha," Burke said, and started the engine.

They parked in front of St. Mary's, tried knocking on the door of the rectory, first.

"Knock again," Burke said. "Mrs. Cox might be upstairs."

"Doing what?"

"Cleanin'?"

"She does all the cleaning *and* the cooking?" Sangster asked.

"Well, yeah," Burke said. "What the heck did you think she did?"

"I thought she was just the cook." Sangster knocked again, louder this time. Still no answer.

"This isn't right," Sangster said.

"Maybe she's in the church."

"Why?"

"Cleaning it?"

"Is that part of her job?"

Burke frowned. "Not that I know of."

"We need to get inside."

"This is a solid door."

"You got lock picks?" Sangster asked.

Burke shook his head. "Never one of my many talents."

"Is the rectory connected to the church? Can we get in that way?"

"I think the buildings are separate."

"Well, there's got to be another door or a window we can use to get in."

"If she's in the church we're gonna feel stupid," Burke said.

"Okay," Sangster said, relenting. "You check the church and I'll try to get in here."

Burke nodded. "I'll meet you back here."

"Fine."

They split up, Burke trotting over to the church, and Sangster moving to the side of the rectory.

Sangster tried several windows, but the old building was solid, including the windows. He reached the back of the structure and tried the rear door, but with the same results.

"Well," he said to himself, "at least this is encouraging. Chances are nobody was able to break in. So where are you, Mrs. Cox?"

He turned and looked at the church.

* * *

Burke entered the church, which was always unlocked. Not a Catholic himself, he still found the interior of St. Mary's very serene and relaxing.

There was no one else there, no one in the pews or at the altar, no one lighting candles. He checked the confessionals and found them empty.

When the door to the church opened he turned to see Sangster coming inside.

"Nothin'?" he asked, his voice echoing.

"I couldn't get inside," Sangster said, approaching him. "I doubt she's inside."

"Then she must be in here."

"Or she went shopping."

"She doesn't go shoppin'," Burke said. "While I was stayin' here with Father Patrick I saw how things run here. They get supplies delivered. Mrs. Cox has a room in the rectory. She hardly ever leaves the building—except to come over here and light some candles."

"Looks pretty empty."

"I looked everywhere out here. We can go into the sacristy, there's a basement, the belfry—"

"Okay," Sangster said. "Let's do this together."

"Suits me. Let's start with the sacristy."

There were two doors to the sacristy, one in front of and one behind the altar. They went to the door in front, found it unlocked.

"If she's in this church somewhere," Sangster said, "hiding, and she hears us—"

"I get it. We should call out to her."

"Right."

They entered the sacristy, saw cabinets that probably

contained the priests' raiments, and probably those of the altar boys, as well. Sangster had sat in on one of Father Patrick's masses just once, thinking he might feel something. He didn't, but he watched the altar boys perform their duties.

"Mrs. Cox," Burke said aloud, "it's Burke and Stark."

"On the other hand, she could be hiding in the church from Frankie Trigger, who might still be here."

"Now you come up with that? Why would he be after Mrs. Cox?"

"Because no one else was here?" Sangster suggested. "Maybe he thought she could tell him where Father Patrick is."

"She can't," Burke said, "but would he believe her."

"Not until he was finished asking."

Burke turned to face him squarely.

"You sayin' you think he took her?"

"No," Sangster said, "I won't think that until we've finished looking."

"Then we better keep going."

They left the sacristy, debated whether they should try the belfry or the basement first. They finally decided to go with the basement, which turned out to be empty—literally. There was nothing down there for her to even hide behind.

They went back up to the stairs that led to the belfry.

"What if we just ring the bell?" Burke asked, pointing to the ropes.

"If she's up there, she'll end up deaf."

"Good point."

"On the other hand, if Frankie Trigger is up there…"

"That might be fun," Burke said. He walked to the

base of the steps and called up. "Mrs. Cox? It's Burke and Stark, ma'am. Are you up there?"

No answer.

"Not there," Burke said.

"Maybe she didn't hear."

"I could yell louder."

"Let's just go up," Sangster said. "You've still got your gun, right?"

"I do. Where's the .38 you took from your visitor?"

"I left it at the house."

"Probably a good idea." Burke looked up the winding staircase. "How many steps do you think there are?"

"I don't know," Sangster said. "I've never been up there."

Burke frowned.

"Don't think you can make it, old man?"

"You go first, youngster," Burke said. "I'll struggle along behind you."

"Suits me," Sangster said, and he started up.

Aware of Burke's heavy breathing behind him, Sangster slowed his pace before reaching the top. He did not expect to find Frankie Trigger up there, but he still wished he'd had Burke pass him his gun before he took the lead.

As it turned out, he didn't need a gun. When he reached the top and turned to look around he saw, beyond the large bell, Mrs. Cox, sitting on the floor with her back to the wall.

THIRTY-FIVE

"What took you so long?" she asked pointedly.

"We called out," Sangster said.

"We?"

Burke came up the steps behind Sangster and looked surprised when he saw Mrs. Cox sitting on the floor.

"There you are," he said. "We called."

"Yes, well," she said, "my legs are a little cramped. I'll need some help standing up."

Both men rushed to her, took an arm and assisted her to her feet.

"It'll be a little while before I can go down the steps," she said.

"That's okay," Sangster said. "We'll wait."

"Can you tell us what happened?" Burke asked.

"A man came to the rectory," she said. "He was looking for Father Patrick. Because of what you all told me, I knew this wasn't good news."

"He could have just been a someone looking for a priest," Sangster said.

"He had a gun."

"He showed it to you?" Sangster asked.

"I saw it," she said, "under his jacket."

"Did you let him in?"

"I slammed the door in his face and ran out the back

door. I figured he'd be chasing me, so I came up here."

"You didn't think he'd look here?" Burke asked.

She shrugged. "I had to hide someplace."

"He wouldn't have been able to get into the rectory," Sangster said. "I just tried a little while ago. It's pretty solid."

"I didn't think of that," she said.

"Well," Burke said to Sangster," you didn't really try very hard."

"Maybe not."

Sangster looked at Mrs. Cox. "Did he come into the church looking for you?"

"I...don't know. I didn't hear him, but then I didn't hear you, either. This is...pretty high."

Sangster looked at Burke.

"What?"

"He wouldn't just give up," Sangster said. "Once he found out where Father Patrick was assigned, he wouldn't just give up."

"So now...what?" Burke asked. "Where is he?"

Sangster shrugged, jerked his chin toward the street. "Downstairs, maybe? Or out there, watching?"

"So if we go out the front door of the church with Mrs. Cox..." Burke said.

"Who knows?" Sangster said. "He might try to kill two of us and make the third tell him where Father Patrick is."

"Or maybe he's gone," Mrs. Cox said, hopefully.

"That would be nice," Sangster said to her. "How are your legs?"

"I think I can walk," she said, moving first one, and then the other.

"Do you have your keys to the rectory?" he asked.

"I do."

"Then let's go back the way you came," he suggested. "Maybe we won't encounter Mr. Trigger."

"Trigger?" she said.

"Frankie Trigger," Burke said.

"Is that for real?" she asked.

"I'm afraid it is," Sangster said.

They started for the steps, still remaining on either side of her to help, if necessary. But they stopped when they heard someone coming up.

THIRTY-SIX

Burke put his hand inside his shirt and rested it on the butt of his gun.

Sangster kept his left hand on Mrs. Cox's arm and his eyes on the stairs.

The steps coming up were even and steady, slowing as they got closer to the top. They did not sound like the footsteps of a man to him.

He put his hand out to Burke to stop him from drawing his gun.

"Wha—" Burke started to ask, but at that moment a head appeared, then shoulders, and then the whole person.

"So this is where the party's at," Roxy Primble said.

They all went back downstairs and over to the rectory, as Roxy told them there was no one loitering about on the street outside.

"If there was," she said, "I would have seen them."

When they were safely inside the rectory, Sangster suggested Mrs. Cox go to her room.

"Nonsense," she said. "I'll put on some coffee."

She walked to the kitchen, a bit unsteadily, but determined.

Sangster turned on Roxy.

"What the hell are you doing here?"

"I went to your house, but you weren't there. I went back to the ferry and saw you and your buddy drive off, so I followed you here. It's not so far, you know."

There was a sound from the kitchen, like somebody dropped a plate.

"I'll check on Mrs. Cox," Burke said, and went to the kitchen.

"You never called me," Roxy said.

"Did that surprise you?"

"Yes," she said, "I thought we had…chemistry."

"So you thought…what? I'd call, we'd sleep together, and then I'd take you on as…my protégé?"

"Wait," she said, giving it some thought, nodding a few times, then saying. "Okay, yeah, that's how I thought it would go."

"Sorry to disappoint you, Roxy," he said, "but I'm in the middle of something."

"A job?"

"I don't do those kinds of jobs anymore."

"Well, whatever kind of job you're doin'," she said. "I could help."

"I want to know how you knew I was here," Sangster said.

"I'm good at following people," she said. "You didn't see me."

He remained quiet. She studied him for a moment.

"Oh, I get it. You're upset that I was able to follow you without you seeing me," she said. "You really are retired, aren't you?"

Retired or not, he hated the idea that he hadn't known he was being followed. That meant there was a possibility that Frankie Trigger could get to him.

"What are you thinking?" she asked. "That it's a wonder you're still alive?"

"Roxy—"

"You need me," she said, "at least until you get your edge back. Either that or you're gonna end up dead before that can happen."

Burke and Mrs. Cox reentered the room with Burke carrying a tray.

"Coffee and cookies," he said. "Is the lady stayin'?"

Sangster looked at Roxy, who smiled and raised her eyebrows at him.

"The lady is staying."

THIRTY-SEVEN

"You're going to have to make yourself useful," Sangster said to Roxy.

"Who do you want me to kill?" she asked.

Mrs. Cox gave her a stern look, then turned away.

"Not that kind of useful."

"What other kind is there?"

"We're actually trying to keep somebody alive," Sangster explained.

"Who?"

"A priest."

She raised her eyebrows. "Are you serious?"

"Why do you think we're in a rectory?"

"Is that what this place is?"

"Of course it is," Mrs. Cox said. "And Father Patrick's life is in danger. Mr. Burke and Mr. Stark are trying to save him."

"I see," Roxy said. "From the fella that you thought was outside?"

"Did you see him?" Sangster asked.

"I did," she said.

"The question is," Burke said, "did he see you?"

"No more than you did."

"I wouldn't count on that," Sangster said. "He's not out of practice like I am."

"You mean...he's on the game?"

"He's supposed to be the best in the game," Sangster said, "but we can talk about that later." He glanced over at Mrs. Cox hoping Roxy would catch on that he didn't want to talk in front of her.

"Okay," she said, with a shrug, "but I know for a fact he didn't see me."

"How can you be so sure?" Burke asked.

"If he had," she said, "he wouldn't have led me back to where he's staying. Didn't you wonder why it took me so long to come up to the tower? I saw him take off as soon as you guys got here, so I followed him. Then I hurried back."

Sangster digested that for a moment, then looked at the ex-sheriff.

"Burke, can you stay here with Mrs. Cox?"

"I don't need a babysitter," the housekeeper said.

"Just for tonight," Burke said, "in case our friend comes back."

"And I suppose I'll have to feed you," she complained, going back into the kitchen.

Burke smiled at Sangster and Roxy and said, "She loves cookin' and she doesn't really care who eats it. I'll be fine. And I've got this." He took the Peacemaker from the back of his belt.

"That thing will blow up in your hand!" Roxy said.

"It's fine," Burke said. "Works like new."

She rolled her eyes. "It's your hand."

"Let's go," Sangster said to her.

"Where?"

"For a ride on the ferry."

* * *

On the ferry Roxy said, "Okay, I know where this guy is staying, but I don't know who he is. You wanna fill me in?"

"He calls himself Frankie Trigger."

Her eyes went wide.

"That was Frankie Trigger? The best hitman in the business?"

"That's what they say, isn't it?"

"Jesus." She looked pale.

"Still think he didn't see you following him?"

They were sitting side-by-side on a bench, their backs to the window. She squared her shoulders and lifted her chin.

"He may be the best killer," she said, "but nobody sees me following them if I don't want to be seen—nobody."

"I hope you're right," he said, "otherwise he'll be waiting for us when we get there."

"You'll see."

When the ferry stopped Sangster drove his car off onto Canal Street.

"Well," he said, "where to?"

"I'm not sure, exactly."

"I thought you said you followed him."

"I did," she said, "but I kept my eyes on him, not on street signs. I'm not sure of the streets we walked on and I grabbed a cab back."

"He walked to his hotel from the ferry?"

"Yes."

"Then he's staying in the French Quarter?"

"Yes."

"All right." He pulled the car over to get out of the

moving traffic, and turned off the ignition. "Describe it to me."

"It'd be better if we walked it," she said.

"You can retrace your steps?"

"I think so."

Sangster got out and looked around. He was parked in a legal spot.

"All right," he said, "get out and let's start walking."

THIRTY-EIGHT

They walked the French Quarter while Roxy got her bearings from buildings that were landmarks to her.

"I remember that one," she said. "Never saw a building like that before."

"That's an entresol house," Sangster explained. "The Spanish experimented with those. The shop is on the first floor, a warehouse on the second, and then that high balcony is outside of the living quarters on the third floor. Houses like that date back to the eighteen-seventies."

"It's beautiful. He walked past that and kept going..."

They walked further and reached Royal Street.

"I know we passed that," she said, pointing.

"That Brennan's Restaurant," he said. In the early eighteen-hundreds it was the Banque de la Louisiane."

"How do you know all this?" she asked.

"I pay attention to my surroundings."

He was actually enjoying the walk because of the long period he'd spent avoiding the French Quarter. Even when he was looking for Frankie Trigger with Burke he had enjoyed it—to a certain extent.

"There," she said, suddenly excited and pointing. "He went in there."

They were on the corner of Royal and St. Louis, and

she was pointing several buildings down on St. Louis.

"That looks like a small hotel, maybe even a B&B," he said.

"That makes sense, doesn't it?"

When Sangster was active and on a job, he never stayed in big, expensive hotels. He preferred small, out of the way places like this one.

"Should we go in and find out?" she asked.

"No," he said. "If you managed to go unseen to this point, you want it to stay that way. Let's go…there." He pointed to a small store that sold beads, on the other side of the street.

"You're interested in beads?"

"Not beads," Sangster said, "but maybe somebody in that shop knows about the building we're interested in."

"Okay, I get it," she said. "We go look at beads."

"Let's go."

They crossed over and entered the shop. It was small and not very busy. There were a couple of people looking at beads on racks that lined the floor, but they went to look at a rack near the front window. Sangster wanted to be able to ask about the building in passing, as if they had just spotted it through the window.

"Hello," a woman's voice said.

They turned to see a young, chic-looking black woman coming toward them, wearing a silk blouse, tight skirt and bright smile.

"Can I help you with something?" He had expected some sort of accent—perhaps Cajun—but she spoke perfect English.

"We're just looking," Sangster said.

"My husband wants to buy me some beads," Roxy said, sliding her arm through Sangster's. "He doesn't want me showing my boobs to get them."

"Well, you're a lucky girl."

"Believe me, I know it," Roxy said. She leaned over and kissed Sangster on the cheek. "But maybe you can settle a bet for us."

"If I can."

"My husband says that building over there has to be some kind of hotel. I say it's a small museum."

"Ha!" the girl said. "You're both wrong. It's a B&B—the expensive kind."

"Well," Sangster said, "that's kind of a hotel. I win."

"Hey, hey," Roxy said, objecting. "Hotels have a lot of rooms. How many rooms in that place?"

"Uhhhhh, eight, I think," she said.

"That's not a hotel," Roxy said to Sangster. "Nobody wins."

"Fine," Sangster said, "nobody wins."

"Well," the girl said, "let me know if you see something you like."

"We're going over to Café du Monde and talk about it."

"But, you didn't even look—"

"Don't worry," Sangster lied, "we'll be back."

Twenty minutes later they were sitting across from each other at Café du Monde with powdered sugar floating in the air between them.

"What do we do now?" Roxy asked.

"I think Frankie's still going to figure his only connection to Father Patrick is St. Mary's, so he's going to go back there."

"So we wait for him?"

"Well, we'll go back there tonight, but I want to be outside of his B&B tomorrow when he comes out, to get a good look at him."

"And follow him?"

"Yes."

"And kill him?"

"No."

"What are you planning to do if not kill him?"

Sangster bit into a beignet and said, "I'm still figuring that out."

THIRTY-NINE

They went back to Algiers and stopped at Sangster's house before returning to St. Mary's.

"Why are we here?" she asked.

"To talk," he said. "Sit, I'll get two beers."

He went inside, came back and handed her a cold bottle, sat across the chess set from her.

She took a swig. "Whataya want to talk about?"

"You."

"What about me?"

"If you're going to work with me, we need to set certain rules."

"Why?" she asked.

"Well...pretty much because I say so."

"No, I mean, why bother?" she asked. "I thought we did good together today. We got the info we needed and we worked seamlessly."

"We got lucky," he said. "In the future, you need to let me take the lead."

"The future?" she asked. "How far into the future?"

"For as long as it takes us to take care of Frankie Trigger and save Father Patrick."

"And after that?"

"We'll talk when the time comes."

"Okay," she said. "Can we talk about something else?"

"Like what?"

"Food," she said. "When do we eat?"

"We'll head back to the rectory."

"Can we stop along the way for some take out? We can bring it to everyone."

"I don't think Mrs. Cox would appreciate that," he said. "I'm sure she's preparing dinner even as we speak."

"Well then, let's get over there."

Burke let them into the rectory.

"Everythin' okay?" he asked.

"Yeah. Here?"

"Fine," he said. "Quiet. Mrs. Cox is making dinner."

They went into the living room.

"You get anythin'?" he asked.

"We found him," Roxy said. "We found Frankie Trigger."

Burke looked at Sangster.

"We know where he's staying," Sangster said.

"So what's next?" Burke asked.

"I'm thinking of getting there early tomorrow, and following him."

"Is that smart?" Burke asked. "I mean, if he's that good, he'll know he's bein' followed."

"He didn't see me," Roxy offered.

"And he doesn't know me," Sangster said.

"How do you know Jimmy Abbatello didn't tell him as much about you as he told you about him?" Burke asked.

"I'm hoping that's not the case."

"That's all?" Burke asked. "Hopin'?"

"I'll be very careful."

"We'll be careful," Roxy said.

"No," Sangster said, "I will. You won't be with me."

"Why not?" she complained.

"Because if we both try to follow him, he might notice," Sangster said.

Roxy frowned, but before she could complain, Mrs. Cox came in and said, "Dinner's ready."

"Let's talk while we eat," Roxy suggested.

"There's nothing more to talk about," Sangster said. "I'm going, you're not."

"So what do I do?" she asked.

They walked to the dining room and sat down.

"I might have something for you," Sangster said. "I need somebody to check on Father Patrick."

"Patrick doesn't know Roxy," Burke pointed out, "and neither does your man, Allemand."

"That's a good point," Sangster said. "Maybe you should go and check on Patrick, and Roxy can stay here and watch over Mrs. Cox."

"Why does she need watching over?" Roxy asked.

"Because she's the only person who could even be perceived as being close to Patrick," Sangster said. "If Frankie was to take her—"

"So I'm supposed to be a babysitter?" she demanded, cutting him off. "That's not a proper use of my talents."

"I agree," Mrs. Cox said from the kitchen doorway. "Whatever this young lady's talents are, I am not in need of them."

They all looked at her.

"You going to hide in the belfry again?" Sangster asked her.

"He didn't find me, did he?" she asked, and went back into the kitchen.

FORTY

After dinner, Roxy was looking for something to drink.

"Try the church," Burke said. "Maybe there's some sacrificial wine."

She made a face. "I think I'll go out to a bar."

Sangster and Burke exchanged a look.

"I'll go with you," Sangster said. "I could use a beer, myself."

"Whatsamatter?" she asked. "Don't you trust me?"

"Maybe I don't want anything to happen to you," Sangster said. "Algiers at night is no place for a young woman alone."

She laughed. "Seems okay to me."

"Come on," Sangster said, grabbing his windbreaker. "We'll go to Old Point."

"Have one for me," Burke said.

"Coffee and cake?" Sangster heard Mrs. Cox ask Burke as he and Roxy headed for the front door.

"Of course," Burke said, happily.

At Old Point they sat outside and had a beer each.

"You're not really gonna make me babysit, are you?" she asked.

"You can do anything else you want, Roxy," he said,

"you just can't come with me."

"Oh."

"But it'll make it harder for us to check on Father Patrick if Burke has to stay with Mrs. Cox."

"Can't you call your man…what's his name?"

"Allemand."

"Yeah, can't you call him?"

"I don't know if he has a cell phone," Sangster said. "He's kind of…old school." He didn't want to tell Roxy that he had given Patrick a burner. He didn't trust her fully yet.

"Then I guess you should've found that out," she said.

She was right. Knowing whether or not Lew Allemand had a cell phone would have been helpful. He hadn't thought to ask, and that was because he was out of practice.

"Look," he said, "I'm not trying to keep you out of play. I really need someone to stay at the rectory with Mrs. Cox in case Frankie shows up. If he does, it would be just you and him."

"You mean, if he shakes you and shows up," she said.

"Yes."

"Well," she said, "you make a strong argument."

Apparently, the idea of taking Frankie Trigger on alone appealed to her. That just told Sangster she was foolish and wasn't ready. As long as he got her to stay in the rectory, she'd be safe.

"Okay then," he said, "tomorrow you'll watch Mrs. Cox, Burke will go and check on Patrick, and I'll pick up Frankie at his B&B and tail him."

"Sounds like a plan," she said.

FORTY-ONE

Roxy spent the night at Sangster's house.

They went there right from Old Point, and he showed her where the guest room was.

During the night he woke, sat up in bed and listened intently. Somebody was moving around inside the house. It took him several minutes to remember he had company, but that didn't necessarily mean it was Roxy out there.

He slipped from bed and grabbed the baseball bat he kept right by it. Barefoot, he stepped into the hall, stopped and listened again. The sound was coming from downstairs. Somebody was moving around.

He slipped down the hall to the guest room, looked inside, saw that Roxy's bed was empty. He went in to put his hand on the sheets, found them warm. It must be her downstairs, but was she alone? Had she perhaps let someone else in? Was her whole demeanor an act, a set-up to take him out?

He had a gun in the house, but it was downstairs. It was the gun he had taken from Dickensley, which he had put in a desk drawer.

Hefting the bat again, he started back down the hall to the top of the stairs. He stood there and listened, trying to determine if there was only one person downstairs or more.

He finally decided there was only one, but he kept the bat with him anyway as he started down the stairs.

When he reached the bottom, he looked around the living room, saw no one. Then he heard something from the kitchen. He moved across the room, listened at the kitchen door, thought he heard something like a spoon or fork against a plate or a cup. He used the bat to push the kitchen door open, swinging it all the way and peering inside.

"Do you know you've got nothing to eat in here?" Roxy asked from her seat at the kitchen table.

"I eat out a lot," he said.

She looked at what he had used to open the door.

"A baseball bat?" she asked. "How unprofessional."

"Depends on your profession," he said. "What did you find?"

She looked down at the plate and pushed the food around with a fork.

"I'm not sure, but it tastes okay cold."

He walked over and sat across from her.

"That looks like the étouffée I had a while back."

"How long is a while?" she asked.

"You don't want to know."

She put the fork down on the plate, pushed the food away got up and went to the refrigerator. She was wearing a tank top and a pair of panties. She had good, well-toned legs and arms.

"Beer?" she asked.

"Sure, why not?" He took a forkful of étouffée and tried it. He didn't think it was too bad for being over a week old.

She turned back from the refrigerator with two bottles, letting the door close behind her.

She handed him one and asked, "Were you looking at my butt?"

"Not just your butt," he answered.

She seemed surprised. "Oh my God, are you flirting with me?"

"No."

She sat across from him, still smiling.

"You are," she said, "you're flirting with me." She sat back so he could see the outline of her nipples against her shirt.

He stared at her.

"When's the last time you had sex?" she asked.

"Do you want to have sex?"

"Actually," she said, "I just want to fuck, very badly. I'm horny as hell, that's why I couldn't sleep. I almost came to your room."

"So, you want to have sex with me."

"Well," she said, rubbing her bare upper arms, and then sipping her beer, "you're here, I'm here, I'm horny."

"Ah," he said, "then it's not me."

"Are your feelings hurt?" she asked.

"No," he said, shaking his head. "Fact is, I could use some sex, myself."

"Mindless, physical contact," she said, as if making the parameters clear. "I'm not the shy looks and secret touches kind of girl. I know what I want, and I know what I need. I need this."

"Right."

"Okay, then," she said, standing up. "Let's go."

He stood.

"Your room or mine?" she asked.

"My bed is better."

"Fine," she said, "lead the way."

"Ladies first."

She grabbed her bottle from the table.

"Let's bring the beer."

She turned and headed for the door to the dining room.

He wasn't sure what she was up to. Was this on the level or was she trying to distract him for some other purpose?

He followed her.

FORTY-TWO

He woke first, the next morning.

Roxy was still in bed with him. He looked over, saw her curled up underneath the sheet...

The night before, when they'd walked into the room, she had turned and stood for a moment, letting him look at her. He'd seen her nipples beneath the shirt in the kitchen, but now they were hard, poking out at him. Slowly, she crossed her arms in front of her, took hold of the bottom of the shirt and pulled it over her head. Her breasts were not large, but well-shaped, like small but firm pieces of fruit and topped with dark nipples. Pulling the shirt over her head made them go taut, but they relaxed when she let her arms fall to her sides, and he was transfixed.

She was eager and undressed him roughly before pulling him to the bed. He was still concerned that there may be more than just sex on her mind, but once they were naked on the bed together and nothing else happened he decided to enjoy her because, truth be told, it had been a while for him, and he needed this just as much as she did...

* * *

He checked the clock on the night table, saw that it was 5:45 a.m. His mental alarm clock was right on the money. He had no idea what time Frankie Trigger would get up, but he doubted it would be this early.

"What the hell—" Roxy said, waking up as he got dressed.

"I'm getting an early start."

She looked at the clock and said, "Ya think?"

"Go back to sleep, but get over to the church before nine," he said.

"Hey, I just thought of somethin'."

"What's that?" he asked, sitting on the bed to put on his shoes.

"How are you gonna recognize him?" she asked. "You need me to come."

"I've got his description," he said. "Jimmy Abbatello's and yours."

"Well," she said, "if you think that's good enough." She was lying on her back with the sheet over her breasts, her arms folded underneath them.

"I'll see you later," he said, "probably at St. Mary's."

He went out the door into the hall with her shouting, "What, no good bye kiss?"

He was walking to his car when the front door opened and she came flying out, wearing her tank top and panties and carrying a gun. He turned as she came toward him. "What the hell—"

She stopped in front of him, reversed the gun so she could offer it to him, butt first.

"You might need this."

It wasn't hers, but the one he'd taken from the private detective, Dickensley.

"No."

"But why not?"

"I told you," he reminded her, "I'm not going to kill Frankie Trigger."

"And what if he wants to kill you?" she asked, exasperated.

"I'll deal with that when the time comes."

She stared at him, then drew the gun back.

"You're still cold, Sangster," she told him. "Maybe you don't kill anymore or you don't wanna kill, but you're still cold. I wouldn't want to be the one who tries to kill you."

She turned and walked back to the house.

FORTY-THREE

Sangster stood next to the sculpture, staring at the B&B across the street. Not sure where he was going to stand when he got there, he'd been surprised to find the gallery open so early.

As he stood there, he wondered why he was assuming Frankie Trigger wouldn't have left the B&B earlier. If he was wrong he could he standing there all day, waiting, while Frankie was already at St. Mary's.

Before returning home the night before from St. Mary's he had given Burke the burner phone in private.

"If you don't find Allemand at the dock, use this to call Patrick," Sangster said, "but I'd rather the burner he has didn't ring. It might give him away at an inopportune moment."

"I'll be careful," Burke had promised.

"You're back."

He turned and saw the beautiful black girl he and Roxy had spoken to the day before. She had an incredible smile.

"Where's your wife?" she asked.

"She wasn't really my wife," he said.

"No?"

"She was playing a joke," he said. "I went along with it. I'm sorry."

"Please," she said, her smile becoming even brighter, "don't apologize. I'm...glad."

He tried to look at her and out the window at the same time.

"But you are interested in that B&B?"

"Yes."

"May I ask why?"

"You can ask..."

"My name is Nicole," she said.

"I'm Stark."

"Are you some kind of a detective, Stark?"

"Some kind of, yes," he said.

"And you're watching for an errant husband?"

"Something like that."

She touched his arm.

"And is this any more true than the story you told me yesterday?"

"Probably not."

She moved her hand away from his arm, took something out of the pocket of her suit jacket, and handed it to him.

"That's my card," she said. "My home number is on the back. When you're finished with whatever this is you're doing, call me."

"I will," he said, pocketing the card.

She smiled and walked away. He turned his attention back to the window.

It was getting near ten a.m. when Sangster started to worry that he'd missed Frankie. Then the front door opened and the hitman stepped out. Sangster knew him right away, not only from Roxy and Jimmy Abbatello's descriptions, but Joe Maniscalco's as well.

He'd only met Roxy a couple of days ago. The same for Abbatello and Maniscalco. None of those people existed for him before that. He certainly wouldn't trust any of them with his life, although Roxy might get a little more leeway. But they had all been on the money with their description of Frankie Trigger. He was a tall, unusual looking man, the kind of ugly that women would find attractive, like a James Coburn or Charles Bronson.

He stopped in front of the door for a few moments, looked in all directions. Sangster stepped away from the window. Frankie was wearing a T-shirt and black jeans, boots, and a light windbreaker to hide his gun.

After satisfying himself—possibly determining that he was not being watched—he turned right and started walking. Sangster had left his car at the ferry since it seemed Frankie didn't have one.

Sangster wondered where the hitman was going; he was heading away from Canal Street. It took only two blocks to find out. He stopped in a small, corner restaurant, took a table in the window, and proceeded to eat a nice, long, leisurely breakfast.

Sangster found a recessed doorway of an abandoned storefront where he could watch from. There was no way to get comfortable except to lean against the wall. Frankie Trigger spent over an hour eating his breakfast. He seemed to chew very precisely and enjoyed every sip of orange juice and coffee. Finally, he finished and paid his check. As he stepped out the door and turned right again, Sangster's stomach growled.

Frankie only walked a couple of more blocks, and then they were in Jackson Square. Sangster was surprised when the hitman sat down and had his tarot cards read by a street vendor. After that he watched a couple of small boys dance on a corner and gave them some coins. Then he walked along the park fence to look at some of the art work.

Sangster was starting to smell a rat.

Why would a man like Frankie Trigger eat a leisurely breakfast, then take a stroll to Jackson Square, have his cards read, and then browse the amateur artwork on display? All this when he was supposed to be on a job.

There was only one answer.

It was only a matter of hours since his breakfast, but at that moment Frankie took a table outside one of the Jackson Square restaurants and ordered a drink. When the waitress came back, Sangster saw that she put two bottles of beer on the table. Frankie Trigger picked up one, and set the other in front of the chair across from him.

Sangster stepped from his doorway, crossed Jackson Square, and sat down across from Frankie.

"It's about time," the man said. "I didn't know how much longer I could take this place."

FORTY-FOUR

"You saw Roxy," Sangster said.

"Is that her name?" Frankie asked. "She's a good lookin' woman. How could I not see her?"

"And me?"

"Never saw you," the other man said, "but I knew somebody was there. No, that's not true. I knew you were there."

"Abbatello?"

Frankie Trigger nodded.

"He called me and told me I'd be competing with you for the hit on the priest."

"How'd you feel about that?"

"Excited," Frankie said. "I'm the best. You used to be. I thought it was…interesting."

"To say the least."

"Was it your plan to follow me to him?" Frankie asked.

Sangster didn't answer.

"That's okay," the other hitman said. "That means you don't know where he is. That puts me one up on you."

"I suppose it does."

Frankie grinned, showing incisors that were pointed.

"Finish your beer, Sangster, and then get goin' back to your girlfriend."

"Not my girlfriend."

"Okay, protégé, then. Between the two of you, maybe you can get to the priest before I do, but I doubt it."

Frankie finished his beer, set the empty bottle down on the table and stood up.

"It was a pleasure," he said. "I've heard a lot about you. I always wondered what happened to you, where you went. Took some time off?"

"Enough, apparently," Sangster said, "to lose my standing."

Frankie Trigger grinned. "Well, it'll be interesting, like I said. I'll be goin' now. Please don't try to follow me again. If I catch you, I'll have to kill you."

"You didn't catch me this time," Sangster pointed out.

"We're mincing words," Frankie said. "Have a good day, Sangster."

"You, too, Frankie. Or would you prefer I call you Mr. Trigger?"

"Naw," the man said, "Frankie will do just fine."

Frankie Trigger squared his shoulders, tugged at the bottom of his windbreaker, and walked away.

Sangster had never picked up the beer. He did now, taking a sip as he watched Frankie Trigger walk across Jackson Square.

Once the hitman was out of sight, Sangster took a burner phone out of his pocket. He had the numbers of the phones he had given to Father Patrick and Burke. He didn't want to call Patrick, unsure where Lew Allemand had hidden him, he didn't want to take a chance of giving the priest away, so he keyed in Burke's number.

"Is that you?" Burke asked.

"Good guess."

"Well, since you're the only one who has this number—"

"Never mind," Sangster said. "I just had a beer with Frankie Trigger."

There was a moment's hesitation, then Burke asked, "And how did that go?"

"Turns out he spotted Roxy, and knew I'd be along, eventually."

"Abbatello?" Burke asked.

"You guessed right, again," Sangster said. "He now thinks we're after the same target."

"Where are you?" Burke asked.

"Jackson Square. How about you?"

"I just left the dock," Burke said. "The boat's there, but not Allemand. Do we know where he lives?"

"No," Sangster said, "but we both know somebody who might."

"Polly?"

"Right."

"I'll go and see her."

"I'll head back to the rectory," Sangster said. "Trigger might be headed there now."

"You guys might be on the same ferry."

"That would be interesting," Sangster admitted.

Sangster retrieved his car from the ferry parking lot, then drove across the Mississippi River Bridge and took General DeGaulle Drive to Algiers. Normally a sixteen-minute ride, but he'd had to retrieve his car, so it took him almost twenty-five minutes to get to St. Mary's rectory. Because of the ferry schedule it was still quicker.

He parked down the street from the rectory, then walked to it, scanning the street and the surrounding buildings. If Frankie Trigger was there, Sangster couldn't see him.

He knocked on the door and it was opened by Roxy.

"I didn't expect you this soon," she said.

"Everything okay?"

"Fine."

He stepped in, locked the door behind him, then followed her in. Mrs. Cox came out of the kitchen.

"Have you eaten?"

"Not a thing," he said.

"I'll fix you something," she said, and walked away.

"How are you two getting along?" he asked Roxy.

"She fed me," Roxy said, "but she won't talk to me."

"Don't feel bad," Sangster said, "she really only talks to Burke."

"Why are you back here?" Roxy asked. "Is Frankie Trigger outside?"

"I didn't see him."

"You didn't follow him here?"

"No, I followed him to breakfast, and then to Jackson Square, where he acted like a tourist for a couple of hours."

"What?"

"Even got his tarot cards read."

She frowned at him. "What's the gag?"

"The gag is, he spotted you," Sangster said. "He finally took a table at a corner restaurant, ordered two beers and just...waited for me."

"Two?"

"One for him," he said, "and one for me."

Sheepishly—because she'd just been told that she'd been made—she asked, "What did you do?"

"I drank it."

FORTY-FIVE

Mrs. Cox brought some leftovers out to the table for him.

"Nothing too exotic," she said. "Just some chicken."

It turned out to be Creole baked chicken with grape tomatoes and yellow bell peppers, among other vegetables and spices.

"Thank you, Mrs. Cox. Is there enough left for Burke when he gets here?"

"Plenty," she said.

She also put a pitcher of ice water on the table for him, then went back to the kitchen.

Roxy sat across from him while he ate.

"What'd you talk about?"

"Him, me. Killing Father Patrick."

"He said he was gonna kill him?"

"Oh, yeah," Sangster said, "but more than that, he said he knew my reputation, and he liked the idea of competing against me."

"So he's not gonna kill you."

"He didn't say he was going to kill me," Sangster said. "Then again, he didn't say he wasn't. But even if he is, it won't be until after he's killed Father Patrick."

"And you're gonna make sure he doesn't do that."

"Correct."

"Can I have some of your water?" she asked.

"Sure."

She grabbed his glass and drank, then refilled the glass for him.

"Nervous?" Sangster asked. "Now that he knows about you?"

"That depends," she said. "What does he know about me?"

"That you're a good looking woman," he said, "and that you're my girl."

"And my name?"

"No," Sangster said, "he doesn't know that."

"Well, that's good."

"But he knows what you look like," Sangster said. "You're going to have to stay with me."

"At your place?"

"Day and night."

"I like the sound of that."

Mrs. Cox cleared her throat from the kitchen doorway. She was regarding them disapprovingly with her arms folded beneath her breasts.

"Mrs. Cox?" Sangster said.

"I'm going to my room, Mr. Stark," she said. "When Sheriff Burke returns, if he wants to eat, he can knock on my door."

"All right," Sangster said. "Thank you."

"You can just put your plate and utensils in the sink when you're finished."

"I'll do that."

As Mrs. Cox moved away, Roxy reached out and snatched a carrot from Sangster's plate.

"Get a plate," he said.

"I ate," she said, taking another carrot. "I think we offended her."

"Probably."

"At least we weren't talkin' about fucking."

"We've talked about that."

"We've done it," she said. "We'll do it again."

"Will we?"

She smiled. "If we're gonna be together day and night, yeah."

He ate one of his carrots while he still had them.

"What are we waitin' for now?" she asked. "Frankie to show up?"

"Burke," he said. "I want to hear about Father Patrick."

"What if he can't find Father Patrick and your friend—what's his name?"

"Allemand," Sangster said. "He was going to ask Polly where they might be."

"Polly?"

"His housekeeper."

"His housekeeper would know?"

"Well," Sangster said, "she's a little more than his housekeeper."

"Ah," Roxy said, "we're talkin' about fucking, again."

"You are," Sangster said, forking a piece of succulent chicken into his mouth.

He was almost finished eating when the front doorbell rang.

"I'll get—"

"Stay where you are," Sangster told her. "I'll get it."

"It's probably only Burke!" she called after him.

As he went to the door, she grabbed the last morsel of chicken off a bone and ate it.

When Sangster opened the door a crack he stood aside, in case someone decided to kick the door in. It was Burke.

"There you are," Sangster said, opening the door wide.

"We've got a problem, I'm afraid," Burke said.

They walked to the dining room and joined Roxy at the table. Sangster sat and pushed his plate away. Burke sat and eyed the plate.

"There's more in the kitchen," Sangster assured him. "Mrs. Cox said you only have to knock on her door."

"Good. I'm starvin', but first—"

"Right," Sangster said. "The problem. What is it?"

"I spent the whole day looking for Father Patrick and Lew Allemand."

"And."

"I couldn't find them anywhere."

"So, Allemand hid him well."

"It could be," Burke said, "but I'm afraid... well...Polly gave me an address for Allemand. It was a house, and when I got there, it was empty."

"Nobody home?"

"I knocked, and when nobody answered I let myself in," Burke said. "Sangster...the place was a shambles. Like there'd been a huge fight. I think maybe Patrick is...gone."

FORTY-SIX

"Okay," Roxy said, "exactly what do you mean by 'gone?'"

"Just that," Burke said. "He wasn't there and neither was Allemand."

"What about the dock?" Sangster asked.

"The boat's there," Burke said, "and that's all."

"What kind of shape is the boat in?" Sangster asked.

"It looks okay," Burke said. "I mean, the same, which is okay...right?"

"It's the way Allemand wants it," Sangster said, "and it floats...right? Still floating?"

"Still floating."

"Okay," Sangster said, "why don't you knock on Mrs. Cox's door...unless you want Roxy to go in the kitchen and get you some food."

"Say what?" Roxy asked.

"I'll get Mrs. Cox," Burke said.

"Okay. Then we'll talk more."

As Burke left the room Roxy asked, "What are you thinkin'? Does Frankie Trigger have him?"

"No," Sangster said. "He can't. No way he knew where Patrick was."

"Why not?"

"Because we didn't know where he was."

Burke came back.

"She'll be right down. So, what do you think? Frankie Trigger has Patrick?"

"No," Roxy said, before Sangster could speak. "He couldn't have known where Patrick was."

"Why not?"

"Because we didn't know where he was."

"Good point," Burke said.

"Besides," Sangster said, "Frankie couldn't have been in two places at once. He was with me this afternoon, while you were looking for Patrick. How could he have found Patrick and had time to go and get him?"

They heard Mrs. Cox in the kitchen.

"So you're sayin' somebody else trashed that place?" Burke asked. "Then where are Patrick and Lew Allemand?"

"I don't know," Sangster said. "Maybe Allemand has his own troubles that we don't know about. Maybe the house was simply burglarized."

"Trashed," Burke said. "I've seen burgled houses, but this place was trashed."

"What about the neighborhood?" Sangster asked.

"It's Treme in the Seventh Ward on the other side of Esplanade. It's always been a Creole neighborhood, and they don't usually do that to each other."

"The key words here being 'don't usually,'" Sangster said. "Do you have any contacts you can ask if that sort of thing has been happening, lately?"

"I can make a few calls," the ex-sheriff said. "That wasn't my bailiwick, but I know some people."

"Okay, do that," Sangster said. "Let's see what we can find out before we start to worry. Did you try calling Patrick's burner phone?"

"I did," Burke said. "No answer."

Sangster took out his own and keyed in the number of the phone he'd given to Father Patrick. He let it ring ten times. There was no answer.

"Okay," he said, disengaging the phone, "now there's a little more reason to worry, but let's not panic."

Mrs. Cox came out with a plate for Burke and set it down in front of him.

"Lemme eat," Burke said, "and then I'll make some calls and find out what's goin' on in the Seventh Ward."

"And what do we do while Sheriff Burke is eatin'?" Roxy asked.

"Well," Sangster said, "one thing, I'd advise you to keep your hands off his carrots."

FORTY-SEVEN

Sangster and Roxy didn't leave the rectory until Burke had made his phone calls. They were in the sitting room having coffee when he entered, carrying his own cup.

"Mrs. Cox turned in for the night," Burke said, sitting with them. "And I made my calls."

"What's the verdict?"

"There's been no history of break-ins for the Seventh Ward just for the sake of doing damage."

"So this is unusual," Sangster said. "That's not good news."

"What can we do?" Roxy asked.

"I've got to see that house," Sangster said.

"That's a good idea," Burke said. "I was alone and didn't spend that much time lookin' around or checking with neighbors."

"Roxy and I will go there tomorrow," Sangster said, "and see what we can find out."

"Frankie might follow us," Roxy said.

"That would be good," Sangster said. "It would mean he doesn't have Patrick. In fact, I'd like him to be outside right now."

"Well," Burke said, "let's go find out."

They put their cups down and walked to the front door. Burke opened it and Sangster and Roxy stepped outside. It was dark, but not pitch black, and there was no sign of anyone lingering across the street.

"Unless he's on a rooftop," Sangster said, "he's not here."

"Then where is he?" Roxy asked.

"I don't know," Sangster said, "but we're not looking for him. Let him find us."

They said goodnight to Burke and started walking to Sangster's house.

"Stop," Sangster said, as they approached it.

"What is it?"

"There's somebody on the porch."

"Frankie Trigger?"

"I don't think so," Sangster said. "Why don't you take a walk to Old Town and I'll come and get you when I'm done here."

"Do you want my gun?"

"No," he said, "I won't need it."

"Do you know who it is?"

"I think so," he said. "I'll see you in a little while."

She turned and headed back toward the Old Town Bar, while he continued on to the house. It wasn't totally dark out. He spotted the car in front and had an idea who was on his porch. As he went up the walk, he saw that he was right.

"There you are, Mr....Stark," Detective Telemaco said.

"Detective," Sangster said, stepping up, "what brings you here?"

"The other night, when I was here, I said we'd talk again," Telemaco said. "I just thought I'd come around and have that talk. That is, unless you're busy…again?"

"Busy?"

"With your girlfriend?"

"I don't have a girlfriend at the moment, Detective," Sangster said, sitting across the chessboard from him, "so I'm free to talk. What's on your mind?"

Telemaco nodded. "So she's not your girlfriend. Fine. We won't argue the point. What was her name? Roxy?"

"That's right."

"So I thought I'd come back, catch you alone, and give you another chance to explain why you rang me."

"I told you," Sangster said. "I made a mistake. I overreacted."

"Now," Telemaco said, "I think you and me, especially after Vegas, know that you never overreact to anythin', Stark."

Sangster studied the man, then said, "I bet you can use a beer."

"I can always use a beer."

Sangster went into the house and returned with two bottles, sat back down across from the detective. The few extra minutes fetching the beers had helped him decide how to play the situation.

FORTY-EIGHT

"What can you tell me about the Seventh Ward?" he asked.

"You mean Treme? Not as prosperous as it once was, but there are still lots of restaurants and halls people use for celebrations. The Autocrat Club is one of the best."

"What about residential neighborhoods?"

"Some homes, lots of the people are still Creole. It's right across Esplanade from the Quarter. It's sure as hell ain't a tourist attraction, though. Why?"

"I've got to go there tomorrow."

"What for?"

"I'm looking for somebody."

"And what's this got to do with why I came here?"

Sangster shrugged and said, "Nothing, I guess. I just thought I'd get some information from you."

"While not givin' me a thing, right?"

"You find out who killed that guy, yet?"

"You know," Telemaco said, "you think you're changin' the subject, but you're not. When I saw you in that hotel down on Canal you were lookin' for somebody, too. Still lookin' for the same person?"

"Not really. This is different."

"Who are you lookin' for this time?"

"A friend of mine," Sangster said.

"This friend got a name?"

"Allemand," Sangster said, "Lewis Allemand."

Telemaco looked stunned. "I'm surprised you answered that question."

"Why?" Sangster asked. "I like to cooperate with the police."

"Yeah, right."

"Where's your partner?"

"Working another angle," Telemaco said. "He's not your biggest fan, so he doesn't like when I come and talk to you."

"What'd I do to him?" Sangster asked.

"He gets a feelin' about people," Telemaco said, "and once he gets it, he never changes his mind. First time he met you, he got a bad feelin'."

"I'm sorry to hear that."

Telemaco put his empty bottle down next to the chessboard. It surprised Sangster, because he didn't recall ever having seen the detective take a swig.

"And now you can answer my original question."

"Which was?"

"Why'd you call me the other night?"

"You're not going to let that go, are you?"

"No."

"Fine," Sangster said. "Somebody was following me, and I wanted to know if you sent him."

"That was it?"

"That was it."

"Is he still following you?"

"No."

"Did you find out who it was?"

Sangster hesitated slightly, then said, "No."

"Now see?" Telemaco said. "We were doin' real

good there for a while, and you were tellin' me the truth. Now you just lied to me."

"It's not important, Detective. Really."

"It was important enough for you to call me," Telemaco said.

"Like I said—"

"You didn't overact!"

"—I made a mistake."

"Just tell me one thing, then."

"Okay."

"Did you kill him?"

"No."

Telemaco studied him for a few moments, then said, "Okay, I believe that. But I also believe you found out who it was and maybe convinced him not to follow you anymore."

"If I did that," Sangster said, "I did it without breaking any laws."

Telemaco stood up. "Okay, that's the truth, too."

"Another beer?"

"No," the detective said, "I got what I wanted. Good night."

As the detective walked back down the path to his car, Sangster wondered if that was the truth.

It was only moments after Telemaco drove away that Roxy came to the house. She sat down across from Sangster in the chair Telemaco had just vacated.

"Your friend, the detective," she said.

"Not my friend."

"What was that about?"

"He still wanted to know why I called him the other night."

"And did you tell him?"

"I did."

"The truth?"

"Close enough."

"Then can we go inside?"

Sangster reached out, picked up the two empty bottles, and said, "We can go inside."

FORTY-NINE

Sangster woke the next morning with Roxy asleep on his right shoulder. It wasn't a position he had ever liked being in. In the past it would have meant that his gun hand was pinned, and he was vulnerable. He wasn't living that life now, but he still felt uncomfortable. He managed to slide free of her and got out of bed.

He took a shower, not concerned about whether or not the noise would wake her up. They needed to get going anyway. He wanted to get to the house in Treme and have a look himself.

The shower did wake her up, because the next thing he knew she was in there with him. The water coursed down her body, pouring off the ends of her nipples as she smiled at him.

"Mind if I share?" she asked.

"You can have it," he said. "I'm done. I'll make some coffee."

"You sure?" she asked, raising her eyebrows. She reached for his cock, which was beginning to harden. Her fingers barely brushed it as he stepped out of the shower stall.

"I don't like sex in the shower," he said, grabbing a towel and drying off.

"Why not?" she asked.

"I've never found a woman I could agree with on the temperature of the water."

"I can see why," she said, reaching for the hot faucet and turning it.

"Coffee," he said, hanging the towel back up.

"Hey, can't I get my own towel?" she called, as he went out the door.

He made toast and coffee, trying to ignore his persistent erection. Roxy was a free and easy girl, sexy as hell, and if there was one thing Sangster wasn't, it was free and easy. It wasn't a lifestyle he could embrace, whether he had a soul or not.

Roxy came in, wearing the same T-shirt and jeans from the day before.

"If this goes on any longer, I'm gonna need a drawer," she said, with a smile, "and a key."

"We'll see," he said. He put a platter of toast on the table, some butter, jelly, and then two cups and a coffee pot.

"I'm impressed," she said. "You can cook."

"This is hardly cooking." He sat across from her, poured them both coffee.

"Is the plan the same?" she asked, buttering her toast.

"It is," he said. "You stay by my side all day, and we go and check out the house in the Seventh Ward."

"And what are we hopin' to find?"

"Something," he said, "to tell us if Father Patrick was there, and if he was, where he went."

"Or where he was taken."

"We'll talk to some of the neighbors, see if anyone

saw or heard anything. And we'll find out if it was actually Lew Allemand's home."

She wrinkled her nose. "Sounds like police detective work."

"There's footwork required in every job," he told her. "You can't just rush in and do a job without checking out the conditions first."

"Yes, sir, teacher."

Sangster parked his car down the street from the address Burke had given him, in front of one of Treme's many halls. They got out of the car and looked around.

"Not too many people on the street," Roxy said.

"I'm sure a lot of them are at work."

As they walked down the street she said, "These homes are real old."

"Some people grow up in a house and then just stay there," he commented.

"Man," she said, "I couldn't wait to get out of the house I grew up in."

Sangster didn't comment.

"I don't suppose you want to talk about your past, growing up," she said.

"Not especially."

"I didn't think so."

They reached the house they wanted and stopped.

"My God!" she said.

"It's a perfectly fine house," Sangster said.

Roxy looked at him, opened her mouth to say something, then thought better of it and simply said, "Yeah, okay."

"Let's go inside."

"How about I check with some of the neighbors—"

"What part of staying with me didn't you understand?" he asked.

"Right, right."

There was a storm door hanging by one hinge and a wooden door that was unlocked. Sangster opened it and went in with Roxy behind him.

The inside was comfortably furnished though—according to Roxy—not tastefully so. However, most of the furniture, save for a chipped coffee table, had been overturned.

"Look around," he said, "see if you can find anything to indicate that Lew Allemand lives here."

"Right. What are you gonna do?"

"I'm going to look for any sign that Father Patrick was here."

"Okay, then," Roxy said, "as long as we both have jobs."

It wasn't a large house, and they started at opposite ends. By the time they joined each other again in the living room, Roxy had some letters in her hand.

"These are addressed to Lewis Allemand," she said. "I found them in one of the bedrooms." She dropped them on the chipped coffee table. "I guess this is where he lives—or lived."

"Lives, hopefully," Sangster said.

"Did you find anything to show that Father Patrick was here?"

"I found this in the kitchen garbage," he said, and dropped a priest's collar on top of the letters on the table.

"Well, well," she said, "so they were both here, and now they're gone."

"How were the bedrooms?"

"Fine," she said. "All neat and tidy."

"Same in the kitchen and basement."

"Whatever struggle there was seems to have taken place here in the living room."

"There's no blood," Sangster said, looking around. "That's the only good sign."

"So, if it was Frankie Trigger," she said, "he wouldn't have taken them, he would have killed them here. There'd be blood."

"And bodies," Sangster said. "No, Frankie Trigger wasn't here."

"So then who came after them?" Roxy said. "And where are they now?"

"I can't imagine Lew Allemand has these kinds of enemies," he said, "but there's somebody who might know."

"Your friend Burke's woman?"

He nodded. "Polly."

"So we go ask her, now?"

"Let's canvas the neighborhood a bit first," he said, "see if anyone saw anything."

"Ohhhh, more police work?" she said, with a wrinkle of her nose.

"Yes."

"Oh, all right," she said. "Let's do it, then."

FIFTY

They stayed together, knocked on doors of the homes to either side of Allemand's and across the street. They found two people who were home, an older woman and a disabled man. The others appeared unoccupied.

"I'm an old woman," the lady said, "home all the time, and I know people think old women spend time lookin' out the window, but I don't. I'm not nosy."

"I understand," Sangster said. "Have you lived here long?"

"Nigh onto fifty years, now. Would you two like to come in for some tea?" she asked.

"Not right now, ma'am," Sangster said. "Do you know your neighbor across the street, Lew Allemand?"

The woman was small, white-haired and wrinkled, but when he mentioned Allemand she suddenly became coquettish.

"Me and Lew," she said, "we know each other a long time—and real well."

"Have you seen him, lately?"

"Not for a day or two," she said. "I think he had a guest in his house and that's kind of odd."

"Why's that, ma'am?"

"He don't have a lot of friends."

"I see."

"Is Lew in trouble?"

"I hope not, ma'am. Thanks for your time."

"Wow," Roxy said, as they walked away from the house, "an old woman who's not an old busybody. Just what we didn't need, huh?"

It took some time for the man to answer the door. They were about to leave when it opened and revealed an older man on crutches, the metal kind that looped around his forearms.

"Sorry," he said, "it take me a while to get to de do', me."

"That's okay, sir," Sangster said, "we're sorry to disturb you."

"Come in, come in." The man backed away to allow them to enter. "I cain't stand for very long. Come on into de livin' room." They followed him as he dragged himself there.

Sangster could see he was once a robust man, but whatever had taken his legs from him must have taken that as well. As the man dropped into an armchair it was apparent how much simply answering the door had taken out of him. There was a small TV across the room showing a black and white movie with the sound turned down.

"I'm sorry you had to answer the door, sir."

"Dat be okay," he said. "I don't mind havin' guests. I don't gets a lot of visitors, me. My name's Willie Beauclaire."

"Have you lived here long, Mr. Beauclaire?"

"Jes' call me Willie. Everybody do. I been here fifty years or so."

Roxy gave Sangster a look, because he'd hit the nail on the head when talking about the neighborhood's tenants.

"Set, set," the man said, "set yerselves down, now, and tell me whatchoo want?"

Sangster and Roxy sat side-by-side on the worn sofa, the cushions not giving their butts much support. On the TV Jimmy Cagney was on top of the world as Sangster recognized the film as *White Heat.*

"We're looking for Mr. Allemand," Sangster said, "your neighbor across the street."

"Did you talk to Marie next door?" he asked. "She and Lewis, dey was real close at one time, if you know what I mean—but dat was mebbe thirty years ago."

"Yes, and she hasn't seen him."

"I ain't talked with Lewis for a few days, me," the man said.

"I see. Do you know anything about him having a guest?"

"Ah knows he had somebody stayin' in his house," Willie said. "Don't know as it was a guest. It was a white fella, though."

"And have you seen much of him?"

"Naw," Willie said, "jes' a glimpse in the window once or twice. I gets groceries delivered from the market, and I gots to let dem in de do', ya know? So's ah drags myself to the door and sees a white fella in Lewis' window."

"Willie, I'm going to level with you."

"Well," Willie said, "I gots to tell ya after all the years I been on dis eart', that'd be refreshin'." The man cackled for a few moments before he sobered and said, "Sorry. You go ahead, now. Refresh me."

"There was some trouble at Lew's house," Sangster said. "He and his guest are gone, and the house has been messed up. Did you happen to hear anything over there?"

"Ya know, we minds our own bidness around here, we do," Willie said. "We're ol' folks, a sometimes ol' folks we gets victimized, ya know?"

"I do know," Sangster said.

"I gots me a gun in da house," Willie said. "Don't nobody bother with me. Lewis, he don' usually spend a lotta time at home. He got dat boat, you know?"

"I do know, down by the dock," Sangster said. "I've been on it."

"If somebody messed wit' his house, chances are dey mighta messed wit' his boat."

"We're going to check that next, Willie. And I know you mind your own business. But I also think you're a good neighbor. I think you've got something to tell me. Willie, do you want some money?"

Willie cackled again, shaking his grizzled head.

"Hell, naw, I don't need your money, me. Ah gots money, mo' den ah needs to get me to de end of mah days. But you right, young fella, I gots sometin' ta tell ya. You listen to me, and maybe you kin help old Lewis out, huh?"

"I'll listen, Willie," Sangster said, "and if I can help Lew out, that's what I'm going to do."

"Den listen close, de bot' of you," Willie said, crooking a finger at them, "because dis is sometin' I only gon' tell ya onc-et."

FIFTY-ONE

"There are some nice homes here," Roxy said, looking out the window as they drove away from Lew Allemand's house and neighborhood.

"Every neighborhood's got good parts and bad parts," Sangster said.

"Not the one I grew up in," Roxy said. "That was all bad. I couldn't wait to get out of that hell hole."

"Where was that?"

Roxy opened her mouth to reply, then stopped, took a breath and said, "Back east. I walked away when I was fifteen and I've been on my own since."

"Well, you apparently haven't done too bad," Sangster said.

"Oh, I was kind of aimless for a long time, but I think I've got my eye on the prize now, thanks to you."

"Me?"

"You're gonna show me the way, Sangster," Roxy said. "You're my mentor."

"Whoa, whoa," Sangster said, "we're together right now so I can keep you alive. That doesn't mean I'm your mentor."

"Yeah, yeah," she said, "we'll see what happens after we're done with Frankie Trigger. Where are we headed now? To talk to the sheriff's girlfriend?"

"I'll talk to Polly when we go back to Algiers," Sangster said.

"So where we goin'?"

"I want to take another look at Lew Allemand's boat."

"Fine," Roxy said. "I haven't seen it yet, at all. Maybe I'll see somethin' you don't."

"Maybe you will."

"Sure," Roxy said, "I'll give you the feminine view."

They drove for a while, and then Roxy said, "What about what the old man told us there at the end?"

"What about it?"

"Do you believe him?"

"What? That Willie saw Papa Legba in Lew's house? And that he thinks Papa Legba took Lew Allemand?"

"And how about...who and what the hell is a Papa Legba?" she asked.

"It's Voodoo."

"I know that much, but who is he and what's he do?"

"What are you, Catholic? Baptist? Jewish?"

"I was raised Catholic, but I lapsed a long time ago."

"Then you'll understand this," Sangster said. "Papa Legba is the Voodoo version of St. Peter."

"Well," she replied, "why didn't you just say that before?"

They parked then walked to the end of the dock, where Lew Allemand's boat was still tied up.

"At least it's still here," she said.

"I'd feel better if it wasn't," Sangster said.

"Why?"

"Because then at least I'd have an idea where they went."

"Where?"

"The bayou."

"Isn't that the swamp?"

"Some of it," Sangster said, "but people live there."

"Let me guess," she said, "Voodoo people."

"Right," he said, not bothering to explain that they weren't called "Voodoo people."

"Does your friend Allemand believe in Voodoo?"

"Everybody who lives here," he said, "believes in it to some extent."

"Even you?"

"Even me," he said, "as of recently."

He stepped onto the boat.

"What are we going to do?"

"I'm going to have a look around," he said. "You keep an eye out here."

"For the law?" she asked. "Voodoo priests?"

"For Frankie Trigger," he said, and went below.

It was a small cabin, where Allemand could sleep or eat, if he wanted to. There were some drawers and cabinets, which he opened and searched, but he found nothing—until the last one.

"What's that?" Roxy asked, as he came up top.

"It's a burner phone," he said. "It was down below, in a cabinet."

"So?"

Sangster took out his similar looking phone and keyed in a number. The phone he'd brought up from down below began to ring.

"Damn it," he said. "This is the phone I gave Father Patrick."

"Tell me," she said, "does Father Patrick believe in Voodoo...even a little?"

They sat in the car by the dock. Sangster did not start the engine.

"What's it mean, Sangster?" Roxy asked. "Why did he leave the phone in the boat?"

"I don't know," Sangster said. "Maybe it's supposed to tell us where he is."

"So we have to figure it out."

Sangster started the engine and said, "And soon."

FIFTY-TWO

Sangster pulled to a stop in front of a house in Algiers.

"Who lives here?" she asked.

"Polly."

"Ah, Burke's cleaning woman."

"Among other things." He took off his seat belt. She started to take hers off. "You wait here."

"Why?"

"Well," he said, "for one thing, I don't think Polly will talk in front of you."

"And for another?"

"Keep an eye out for Frankie Trigger."

"You really think he could show up?"

"He's the best, isn't he?"

He got out of the car.

"I don't know," she said. "Is he?"

He turned and headed up the walk to the front door. It was a simple A-frame house, old but well kept, especially on the inside, where Polly lived with her two teenage daughters, Octavia and Isola, and her young son, Hugo.

He knocked on the door, wondering which of the kids would answer it, but when it opened he was looking at Polly.

While at work, Polly Bourque wore shapeless dresses

and covered her head with headbands or kerchiefs. But when she was home—or with Burke—she dressed more casually, blouses and jeans mostly, and she was an attractive Jamaican woman in her fifties. Although Burke was in his eighties the age difference didn't seem to be a problem for them.

"Mistuh Stark," she said, "whatchoo doin' here?" Her eyes went wide. "Is Burke all right?"

"Burke's fine, Polly," he said. "I just need to ask you some questions about a friend of yours."

"What friend o'mine?" she asked.

"Lewis Allemand."

"Is dere sometin' wrong with Lewis?"

"Can I come in?"

She stretched her neck to look past him.

"Who dat lady in your car?"

"Just somebody who's helping me with a...problem."

"Dat what you wan' to talk to me about, dis problem?"

"That's right."

"Well den, you have dat lady come in and I make bot' of you some tea and we talk."

"That's okay," he said, "she can stay in the car—"

"Dat rude," she said. "Burke never tol' me you a rude man, and I ain't a rude woman, so you gets her and I make de tea."

She turned and went inside, leaving the door open for him and Roxy.

He walked to the car and waved at Roxy to come out.

"What's goin' on?" she asked, getting out and closing the door behind her.

"She says I'm being rude, leaving you in the car. She wants to make us some tea."

"Well," Roxy said, "isn't that nice?"

They went up the walk and into the house. Sangster closed the door behind them.

"You have a seat," Polly called from the kitchen. "I be right out."

The house was small, in some disrepair on the outside because of its advanced age, but the inside was clean and neat. The furniture had seen better days, but was by no means worn out.

"Kinda nice," Roxy said. "Homey."

"Yes."

"Has she got kids, this Polly?"

"Two teenage girls and a ten-year-old boy."

"Where are they?" Roxy asked. "It's real quiet in here for a house with three kids."

When Polly came into the room carrying a tray with tea and three cups, Sangster could see that Roxy was surprised. Since she knew Polly was Burke's woman, she probably expected an older-looking woman.

"Polly, this is Roxy," Sangster said. "Roxy, meet Polly."

"Miss Roxy," Polly said.

"Thank you for invitin' me in," Roxy said. "And please, just call me Roxy."

He was surprised how polite and respectful Roxy sounded.

Polly put the tray down on the dining room table they were seated at.

"That smells wonderful," Roxy said.

"Dis Jamaican hot tea punch," Polly said, sitting down. She poured for the three of them. "It got tea, orange, lemon, and some rum and brandy, all mixed together."

Roxy took a cautious sip, since it was obviously hot, and her eyebrows went up.

"Wow," she said, "this is delicious."

"And dese," Polly said, pointing to the plate of cookies she'd brought out with the tea, "be Jamaican spice chip cookies. I make dem myself."

Roxy picked one up and took a bite.

"Dat got coconut, ginger and rum, with dark chocolate chips. My kids love 'em."

"Where are the kids, Polly?" Sangster asked.

"Jamaica," she said. "Dey visitin' famly."

Sangster wondered if he was keeping Polly and Burke apart by using Burke so much on this job.

"You drink some tea," she said to Sangster.

"Yes, ma'am," he said, and sipped it. Roxy was right, it was good. He picked up a cookie and bit into it before Polly could tell him to do so.

"What wrong with Lewis?" she asked.

"Has Burke told you anything about Father Patrick?" he asked.

"Burke don't tell me none of yo's bidness, Mr. Stark," she said.

He didn't know whether or not to believe her, but if that was the way she wanted to play it, fine.

"Father Patrick's in danger, Polly, and Burke and I are trying to help him."

"And Miss Roxy, here?"

"Yes," he said, "Roxy's helping, too."

Roxy's mouth was full of cookies so she said nothing.

"We had to hide him, so we brought him to Lewis and asked him to do it."

"Lewis gots lots of place to hide," she said.

"Well, that's what we need to know," he said, "because we can't find them. We need to know where Lewis might have taken him."

"If Lewis hidin' somet'in'," she said, "or somebody, you ain't gon' find it."

"Well, there's a little more to it than that," he said. "We went to Lewis' house in Treme, and it's been ransacked."

"Somebody mess wit' Lewis' house?"

"They did."

She thought a moment.

"What about his boat?"

"His boat's fine," Sangster said, "but we found Father Patrick's cell phone there, so we can't call him."

"Why'n't you call Lewis' cell phone?"

Sangster looked at Roxy, who raised her eyebrows.

"We didn't know he had one," he admitted. "Do you have his number, Polly?"

"I do."

"Will you give it to us?"

"You gots to tell me mo'," she said.

"About what?"

"Lewis' house. De neighbors, dey see or hear anyt'in'?"

"Well, as a matter of fact, the man across the street did say he saw something, but—"

"What he see?" she asked.

When he looked at Roxy, she raised her eyebrows and shrugged.

"He said that he saw Papa Legba in Lewis' house."

FIFTY-THREE

"I wish you came to me before you went to Lewis," Polly said, shaking her head.

"Why?" Sangster asked.

"Lately," she said, "Lewis been sayin' he's been seein' Papa Legba."

"Great," Sangster said.

"So he's seein' things?" Roxy asked.

Polly looked at Roxy.

"Some say dey think dey see Papa Legba," she said, "and some say dey *see* Papa Legba. Lewis, he don't t'ink, he know."

"Okay, so wait," Sangster said, "what does this mean?"

"It mean," Polly said, "you bein kinda selfish, right now."

"Ooh," Roxy said, "snap."

"So you're telling me he really saw Papa Legba," Sangster said.

"I tellin' you he know he saw Papa Legba."

Sangster frowned in frustration.

"So he's not a nut job?" Roxy said to Polly.

Polly scowled at Roxy. "You got no respec', girl."

"Hey, I'm sorry," Roxy said, "I'm just tryin' to get to the point."

"Okay, just sit back a minute," Sangster said to

Roxy. "Polly, where would Lewis be right now? Where would he have taken Father Patrick—who, by the way, as a Catholic priest is not going to believe Lewis saw Papa Legba."

"If he wit' Lewis Allemand when he saw Papa, then yo' priest saw him, too."

"Regardless of that," Sangster said, "his house is trashed, and his boat is still at the dock. Where would they go?"

"Lewis would go somewhere you already been," she said.

"And where's that?"

"Bayou St. John."

"Houngan Henry?" Sangster asked.

Polly nodded.

"If Lewis t'ink Papa Legba after him, he go to Houngan Henry for help."

"Okay, wait," Roxy said, putting both hands up like a traffic cop, "what the heck is a houngan?"

"A Voodoo priest," Sangster said.

"Only a houngan could talk to Papa Legba and get Papa to leave Lewis alone."

"And we're goin' to see Houngan Henry...in the swamp," Roxy said.

"The bayou," Polly said.

"And how do we get there?"

Polly looked at Sangster.

"He left you his boat," she said. "He know you know how to get there."

"I was there once," Sangster said. "That doesn't mean I know how to get back there."

"Den you better t'ink back," she said, "and remember or you ain't gonna find Lewis or your priest."

FIFTY-FOUR

As they were walking to the boat at the end of the dock Roxy said, "This sounds crazy, you know."

"I know."

"Papa Legba, Houngan Henry, and you're drivin' a boat into the bayou?"

"I know," he said, again.

"I mean, do you even know where you're goin'?"

"No," Sangster said, "we'll just figure it out as we go."

"And if your friend Allemand left us the boat, how did he and Father Patrick get to this bayou?"

"Well," Sangster said, "you can drive partway there and then walk—"

"Jesus!" she said. "At least we're not doin' that."

Sangster didn't bother telling her that they could only make part of the trip in Lewis' boat, and then they'd have to switch to a rowboat and row through the swamp full of 'gators. If she knew that, she might prefer the walk. In point of fact, Sangster himself might have preferred the walk, but he'd never gone that way. He'd only been out there once and it was going to be challenging enough for him to remember the route.

When they got to the boat, Roxy stopped short.

"Why don't we call Allemand's cell phone?" she asked. "Polly gave you the number."

"We tried," Sangster reminded her. "There's no cell service on Bayou St. John."

"Then why did Father Patrick leave us his phone on the boat?"

"I think he and Lew were telling us to use it," Sangster said, untying the line holding the boat to the dock, "and that's what we're going to do."

"Do you even know how to drive this thing?"

"I've watched Lew do it," Sangster told her.

"That doesn't really answer my question."

"Get on the boat, Roxy," he said, "or stay behind and wait. Maybe you'll find Frankie Trigger—or maybe he'll find you."

At the mention of Frankie Trigger's name she hurriedly got onto the boat.

Sangster studied the instruments for a moment, then started the engine and pulled away from the dock.

"See?" he said. "Nothing to it."

She did not look reassured.

When they reached the rickety dock Sangster remembered, the row boat was tied up there.

"What are we doin' here?" she asked.

"From here we take the rowboat."

"Why?"

"The water's too shallow for one. That's a pirogue," Sangster told her. "It has a flat bottom."

The dock was just floating there; Sangster helped Roxy so she wouldn't fall into the water.

When they were seated in the pirogue he picked up the oars. For most of the trip he'd be able to row. Where the bottom of the swamp became very shallow, he'd have to use one of the oars as a pole.

"Jesus," Roxy said, hunching her shoulders and looking around at the insects that were flying about.

"Take it easy," he said. "This won't take too long."

As Sangster maneuvered the pirogue through the swamp, he thought about Frankie Trigger. Where was the hitman, and what was he doing at that moment? If he went back to the church rectory and made a concerted effort to get inside, get to Burke and Mrs. Cox, the ex-sheriff would never be able to handle him. If Burke got killed while he was out here in the bayou, looking for a houngan and Papa Legba, he'd never forgive himself.

"You said this wouldn't take long," Roxy complained, smacking a mosquito on her arm. "It's already taken too long. What's that?"

"Sit still," Sangster said. "It's a 'gator."

"An alligator?"

"Yes."

"Omigod!" She stared into the water as the gator glided past them. "Are there more?"

"For sure."

"Jesus Christ," she said, "what are we doin' here?"

"You said you wanted to come."

"You said I had to stay with you," she commented. "You didn't say anything about alligators."

Suddenly, Sangster remembered the 'gator who lived out in Bayou St. John, outside of Houngan Henry's hut.

Houngan Henry had named it Papa Legba.

FIFTY-FIVE

When they reached the Bayou St. John dock it was as rickety, or more so, as the one they had retrieved the pirogue from. Sangster had to assist Roxy, who by this time was deathly afraid she was going to be eaten by an alligator.

Once he got her on dry land her shoulders came down, but only slightly.

"They don't come up on land, do they?" she asked.

"Sometimes."

"What?"

"There's a big one lives around here," Sangster said, finally deciding to tell her. "Houngan Henry calls him Papa Legba."

"Is that a coincidence?"

"To tell you the truth," he said, "I don't know."

"Well, where is he?" she asked, looking around.

"Somewhere," Sangster said. "We'll just watch our step and stay out of the water and the brush." He started to lead the way.

"Christ," she said, "I'm glad I've got a gun."

He turned on her and pointed his finger at her. "Don't pull that thing out unless I say so. Got it?"

"Yeah, I got it."

"The shack is over this way."

Sangster was surprised he'd gotten them this far.

Now he just hoped this was the right place, and that the shack was the right one.

"What was that?" Roxy blurted, jumping as they reached the door.

"Relax," he said, "it's something in the brush. We only have to worry if it comes out."

Sangster remembered the last time he had come here he'd been rowing toward a light which had been emanating from the shack. Now there was no light, despite the darkness. It wasn't pitch black, there just wasn't much sunlight getting through the overgrown swamp.

He knocked on the rickety door and shouted, "Houngan Henry! It's..." Had he told the houngan that he was Stark or Sangster? He couldn't remember.

And then he did.

"...Sangster," he said. "It's Sangster. I was here a few months ago—"

"Come in!" a voice called.

Sangster looked at Roxy, who was glancing around, nervously, holding her purse close to her. He assumed her gun was in there. Still, the purse seemed absurd here in the bayou.

"Remember," he said, "no gun."

"Yeah, right."

He remembered the door opened outward, so he pulled. It creaked, as it had months ago.

They entered.

He expected to find Houngan Henry sitting inside, but instead they saw Father Patrick. Why did that surprise him? Hadn't they come out here hoping to find him, alive?

"Patrick."

"Sangster," Father Patrick said.

"Where's Houngan Henry? And Lew Allemand?"

"They're both here," Patrick said, "just not here-here right now." He looked past Sangster. "Who's your friend?"

"This is Roxy," Sangster said. "Roxy, meet Father Patrick."

"So you're the one this is all about," she said.

Patrick was sitting at a wooden table that hadn't been there last time Sangster was. That one had probably fallen apart and been replaced by this hastily built specimen, which seemed to be leaning to one side because one leg was shorter than the other three.

"What's going on, Patrick?" Sangster asked.

"Beats me," the priest said. "You told me to stick with Lew Allemand. So I stuck, and ended up here with his Voodoo priest."

"But, what happened at his house?" Roxy asked. "When we got there it was a mess."

"I-I'm not sure," Patrick said. "I was in another room. When I heard the noise I came out, found Lew on the floor."

"What did he say happened?"

"He wanted to get out of there, fast," Patrick said. "It took me a while to slow him down long enough to find out what happened."

"What did he say?"

"He said," Patrick answered, "that Papa Legba had come for him, and he'd fought him off. He said we had to get out of there."

"Lew was upset?" Sangster asked.

"Upset? He was panicked!"

"I've never seen Lew Allemand even mildly annoyed," Sangster said. "I can't imagine him panicked."

"Well, he was," Patrick said. "We went to his boat, and then he suddenly decided not to use it. Did you find my phone?"

"I did. On the boat."

"Yeah, I left it there hoping you'd find it and then us. I never thought Lew was gonna take us into the bayou."

"Patrick," Sangster said, "where are they?"

"All I know is they told me to stay inside, no matter what. They said Papa Legba was out there."

"The Voodoo Papa Legba?" Roxy asked. "Or the alligator one?"

Patrick looked at her and said, "Both!"

FIFTY-SIX

"What's goin' on?" Roxy asked, flapping her arms helplessly. "What are we doin' out here?"

"That's what I've been wonderin'," Patrick said. "Can we go back?"

"Not until I talk to Lewis," Sangster said. "I need to know if you guys were really running from Papa Legba or if Frankie Trigger had something to do with this."

"If Frankie Trigger was here don't you think we'd know it?" Roxy asked. "I mean, he's from Philly. He wouldn't exactly be comfortable out here."

"You've got a point," Sangster said.

"Damn straight," Roxy said.

"Still," Sangster said, "we're here. We might as well wait a while." He looked at Patrick, "When did they leave?"

"This mornin'."

"Did they say when they'd be back?"

"Actually," Patrick said, "the Voodoo priest said they'd be back when they had 'exorcised' the demon and Lewis was safe to go back to his life."

"Oh great," Roxy said. "Who knows when that will be?"

"We'll just have to wait," Sangster said.

"I can't afford to," Roxy said, and took out her gun.

"Roxy," he said, "I told you, no guns."

"Unfortunately for you, Sangster, you're not callin' the plays anymore."

Sangster noticed that she wasn't pointing the gun at Patrick, but at him.

"Roxy—"

"I didn't want to do this until we got back to New Orleans with the priest," she said, "but I'll have to kill him here and then have you take me back."

"And then what?" Sangster asked, "You kill me? Why would I bother taking you back? You might as well kill me here."

"Wouldn't you rather have the extra time alive between here and there?" Roxy asked.

"No," Sangster said, "I'm not one of those people who wants to hang onto every minute of life possible. If you're going to kill me, kill me here...then get yourself back to the Quarter."

"I—I can't go back on that boat alone," she said.

"Then you shouldn't have made this play now."

Roxy stared at him, shifting her feet nervously. Suddenly, she pointed the gun at Patrick.

"Hey!" the priest blurted.

"I might as well kill him," she said, "that's what I came to town to do. I'll worry about the rest of it after."

"Sangster—" Patrick said, but Roxy pulled the trigger, making him flinch.

There was the sound of an impotent *click!*

Roxy pulled the trigger two more times.

Click!

Click!

Sangster took his hand out of his pocket and showed her the bullets in his open palm.

"I unloaded your gun hours ago, Roxy" he said.

"Geez!" Patrick said.

Roxy looked surprised, then made a dash for the door.

"Where are you going to go?" Sangster shouted.

She stopped before opening it, realizing Sangster was right.

He walked over to her, took the gun from her limp hand as she hung her head. The bullets went back into one pocket, the gun into the other.

"Just relax, Roxy," he said. "We're going to be here a while."

FIFTY-SEVEN

Sangster found another chair and made Roxy sit in a corner.

"Why don't you tie her up?" Patrick asked. "She obviously wants to kill me."

"She's got nowhere to go," Sangster said, "and she has no weapon."

"Still…" Patrick said, not satisfied.

"Just relax," Sangster said, then walked over to where Roxy was sitting, staring at the floor.

"So are you working with Frankie?" he asked.

"What? Jesus, no. I was after this for myself," she said. "I knew if I could beat you and Frankie Trigger to the target, I'd make a name for myself."

"Wait a minute," Patrick said to Sangster. "Didn't you go to Philly and pretend to be a hitman to get in to talk to Jimmy Abbatello. So why would she think beatin' you to me would make her name?"

"We'll talk about that later," Sangster said, keeping his attention on Roxy. "So all that stuff about learning from me was just a bunch of bullshit?"

"Pretty much," she said.

"But are you really Primble's daughter?"

"Oh yeah, that's true," she said. "That's how I knew everythin' about you, from his records."

"We're going to have to talk about those records and where they are sometime," he said.

"Sure," she said, "if you don't kill me."

"Why would I kill you?"

"Of course you won't kill her," Father Patrick said, "but you will turn her over to the police."

"And why would I do that?" he asked the priest.

"Well...she's a hit...person, isn't she?"

Sangster turned and looked at Patrick.

"There's more to it than that, Patrick," he said. "Just let me handle this. In fact, just stay here. We're going to step outside."

"We are?" Roxy asked.

"Yes." Sangster grabbed her arm and pulled her to her feet. "Come on."

He dragged Roxy to the door and took her outside, closing the flimsy thing behind them.

"What about the 'gator?" Roxy asked, looking around.

"We're not going far," he said. "Look, I don't want to kill you or turn you over to the police. You tried to do a job and I stopped you. I can't fault you for that."

"So you'll let me go?"

"Yes," he said, "but only after this is over. For now I need your word you won't try anything like that again."

"You have my gun," she reminded him.

"You're resourceful," he said. "I want you to give up the thought of killing Father Patrick for the Abbatello contract. I'm committed to saving him from that, and I don't want you getting in my way...again."

"Okay," she said, "but you have to promise to take me out of here."

"We'll go, don't worry," he said. "As soon as Lewis and Houngan Henry get back."

"Can we go back inside?"

"Sure."

"Wait," she said, grabbing his arm. "How did you know to take the bullets out of my gun?"

"I was suspicious, Roxy," he said, "when you wanted to have sex. It was too obvious a way of getting close to me, gaining my confidence."

"Why couldn't you just believe I was attracted to you?" she asked.

"Please," he said, and opened the door.

They went back inside.

FIFTY-EIGHT

Patrick had been there long enough to know where things were, so he made some tea for the three of them.

"Is this some kind of Voodoo tea?" Roxy asked, as he handed her a cup.

Patrick laughed. "I asked the same thing." He sipped his. "It actually isn't bad."

Roxy took a tentative sip, then took another. "Not bad," she agreed.

Sangster drank his tea and stared out one of the grungy windows.

"Anythin'?" Patrick asked him.

"No, nothing."

Patrick went back to the chair he'd been sitting in, which was across the room from where Roxy was seated. It seemed wise to keep that much space between them.

"Are we gonna have to sleep here?" Roxy asked.

"I don't know," Sangster said. "Do you think you could sleep here?"

"Not a wink," she said.

Sangster looked at Patrick.

"How long have you and Lewis been here?"

"A couple of days, I think."

"You sleep?"

"I had to, eventually," he said. "I was just too tired."

"See—" Sangster started, turning back to Roxy, but he stopped when he saw that she had fallen asleep in the chair. The cup in her hand was empty.

"It's the tea," Patrick said. "It has that effect."

Sangster looked at his own cup, which was still half full. He set it down on the unsteady table.

"Thanks for the warning."

There were only the two chairs in the cabin, but there was also a pallet that Houngan Henry slept on. Sangster sat on it, his back to the wall. Roxy continued to doze, and Patrick even nodded off, but Sangster kept himself awake by thinking about Frankie Trigger. Once he got Patrick, Roxy and himself off Bayou St. John and back to civilization, he'd have to find someplace else to hide the priest. Apparently using Lew Allemand had not been the best idea he'd ever had. And once Patrick was hidden again, Sangster was going to have to make some decisions about what to do with Roxy, how to handle Frankie, and how to get Jimmy Abbatello to remove the contract from Patrick's head.

Sangster never quite fell asleep, but he was drifting off when he suddenly heard something outside. He sat up on the pallet and strained to hear. Was it the 'gator, Papa Legba? Or something else?

He got up and moved to the window, tried to see through the grime. Two figures were approaching the shack. He thought about taking Roxy's gun out and loading it, but decided against it. He turned to face the door and waited.

Seconds later the door opened and the two figures entered: Houngan Henry and Lew Allemand. Allemand looked the worse for wear, while the Houngan appeared unaffected by their sojourn into the swamp.

The old Cajun looked at Sangster in surprise, while Houngan Henry betrayed no such emotion.

"Tea," he said, and walked to the stove.

Patrick and Roxy came awake from their opposite sides of the room.

"Wha—" Roxy said, rubbing her eyes.

"Lewis!" Patrick said. "Are you all right?"

"I'm fine, me," Allemand said. He looked at Sangster. "What you doin' here?"

"Lookin' for the two of you," Sangster said.

"How you know to look here?"

"Let's call it a hunch."

Allemand looked at Patrick.

"All I did was leave my phone on your boat," the priest said. "He guessed the rest."

"We saw the mess at your house," Sangster said, "and talked to your neighbors."

"My neighbors?" Allemand said. "Dey know not'in'."

"That's pretty much what we found out," Sangster said. "Except for some stuff about Papa Legba."

Allemand shuddered at the mention of the name.

"Papa came for Lewis," Houngan Henry said.

"The 'gator?" Roxy asked.

All the men looked at her, but no one replied to the question.

"So what happened?" Sangster asked.

Houngan Henry had the pot going, then turned to address the room.

"I convinced Papa Legba that Lewis was not ready to cross over."

"You can do that?" Patrick said. "I mean...that's within your...power?"

"It is not a power," Houngan Henry said, "it was only a conversation. After all, do you not talk to your God?"

Patrick stared at him, then said, "I guess so. I mean, I've never obviously had a back-and-forth conversation with God, but...I suppose I see your point."

"Are you serious?" Houngan Henry asked. "You are a priest and you have never spoken with your God?"

"No, I have," Patrick said, "I mean, I've spoken *to* him, just not...*with* him."

"Perhaps you have simply not reached that plain of existence within your religion?" Houngan Henry suggested.

"Your pot is boiling," Father Patrick said.

"Lewis," Sangster said, "why didn't you call me and let know what was happening?"

"You tell me to keep the priest wit' me all de time and not call you," Allemand pointed out.

"Yes, but, in case of an emergency—"

"Wasn't no emergency," the older man insisted.

"Your house looked like a hurricane hit it."

"Dat was Papa Legba," Allemand said. "Was no emergency. I knowed Houngan Henry could help me."

"How'd you know that?" Patrick asked.

Allemand looked at the priest and said, "I have fate."

"Faith?" Roxy asked.

"Dat right," Allemand said. "Fate."

FIFTY-NINE

Sangster could see that Patrick was shaken. He just wasn't sure by what. Was he worried about Frankie Trigger finding him or was he having some sort of crisis of faith? Both Lew Allemand and Houngan Henry seemed to have unshakeable faith in the Voodoo priest's ability to bargain for Allemand's life with Papa Legba. Could Father Patrick ever do the same thing with his God? And did what Houngan Henry had done have anything to do with a soul, Sangster wondered?

"Okay," he said, "I think we're done here. Lewis, do you want to come back with us?"

"Are you takin' Father Patrick?" he asked.

"I am," Sangster said. "He's no longer your responsibility."

"You use my boat to get here?"

"I did."

Allemand made an unpleasant face.

"Don't worry," Sangster said. "I can get it back to your dock without any damage."

"Den I stay a while longer wit' Houngan Henry."

"That's up to you," Sangster said. "I appreciate your help, and I'm sorry if I caused you any trouble."

"No trouble," Allemand said. "Papa Legba woulda come if Patrick dere or not."

"Yeah," Sangster said, "right."

* * *

They worked their way through the swamp in silence, Roxy too scared to talk, Patrick busy with something he didn't want to discuss. It didn't change until they were on Allemand's boat out on Lake Pontchartrain.

Roxy sat at the stern, staring out at the water, her hair blowing in the wind.

Patrick came up next to Sangster on the small bridge.

"You look like a natural," he said.

"This is only my second time driving this thing," Sangster said.

"It doesn't show."

Patrick stared out at the water.

"What's on your mind?" Sangster asked.

"You know all those questions you asked me about a soul?"

"Yup."

"I never helped you very much, did I?"

"It's my problem."

"Yeah, but I'm supposed to be helpin' people figure things out," Patrick said. "Now I can't even help myself."

"With what?" Sangster asked. "What's going on?"

"I think I'm havin' a crisis of my own, Sangster."

"A crisis?"

"Of faith."

"Oh." Sangster didn't think he'd ever had a crisis of faith. Although he'd discovered he had a soul, it hadn't driven him to any specific religion, and certainly not to any sort of deity. Not yet, anyway.

"I mean, listening to Houngan Henry talk about conversin' with Papa Legba—"

"You didn't believe all that, did you?"

"That's not the point," Patrick said. "He believes it, Lewis believes it—you know, at the house? It was Lewis who tore it up."

"What? He did that to his own house?"

"I heard the noise, came down, and there he was, trashin' it," Patrick said. "When I asked him what was goin' on he said that Papa Legba had come to him. I asked what we could do, and he said we had to go and see Houngan Henry. He explained that he was a Voodoo priest, so I agreed to go. When we got there they started talking about Papa Legba and it sounded like nonsense to me, but they really believed it. And then, when they got back and Houngan Henry said he'd conversed with Papa, and asked if I had ever conversed with my God…it made me stop and think. What makes my religion more viable than theirs? Than any other?"

"Who says it is?"

Patrick hesitated, then said, "In the seminary, they teach us that God is the one true God, and our religion is the one true religion."

"That's ridiculous," Sangster said. "They teach that to Catholic priests?"

"They do?"

"And you believe it?"

"Well…I was older than my fellow students," Patrick said. "I had questions in my mind, but I didn't ask them. Not then."

"But you're asking them now?"

Patrick nodded. "I don't know if I can go back, Sangster."

"Well, Fath—Patrick," Sangster said, "first we have to make sure you stay alive to make that decision."

"No," Patrick said, "I think I should remove that burden from you, Sangster. You have your own questions to answer."

"What do you mean?"

"I mean I should leave New Orleans," Patrick said. "Start runnin'. Get away from Frankie Trigger, Jimmy Abbatello, everything about Philly."

"But...they'll probably find you again, Patrick," Sangster said. "Like they did this time."

"I don't know what else to do, Sangster."

Sangster thought a minute, then said, "I think I do."

SIXTY

"You want me to what?" Roxy asked, when they got back to the dock.

"Kill Father Patrick," Sangster said.

"But...but that's what you're tryin' to keep from happenin'," she said.

"I don't mean for real," he said. "I want you to go to Philly, to Jimmy Abbatello, and tell him you killed Patrick. Collect your bounty. Make your name, if that's what you really want to do."

"It is...I think," she said.

"Look," Sangster said, "if you do this everybody wins...and then you can decide what you want to do later."

"Frankie Trigger doesn't win."

"He's a professional," Sangster said. "Once Jimmy tells him the job is done, he'll move on to his next job."

"Are you sure?"

"That's what I'd do—or what the old me would have done," Sangster said. "A job's a job, Roxy. There's nothing personal about it."

"You sure have got a lot of faith in a killer," Roxy said. "Two killers, for that matter."

"I used to be a killer," Sangster said, "so I guess I've got faith in three." He looked to the end of the dock, where he'd told Patrick to walk to and wait. "Nice to know I've got faith in something."

"Okay, so how am I supposed to prove I killed Father Patrick?" she asked. "Jimmy ain't gonna pay without proof."

"Well, we might need some help there."

"Help from who?"

"From somebody Jimmy *would* believe."

"Who, you?"

"No," Sangster said, "I'm sure he wouldn't believe me at all."

"Frankie?"

"I don't think we could get Frankie to go along with this."

"Then who?"

"I was thinking he might believe a cop."

"A cop?" she asked. "You mean that detective friend of yours? Why would he go along with this?"

"He's all about keeping the peace in New Orleans," Sangster said. "That's what we'd be doing."

"This I gotta see," Roxy said.

For want of a better place they returned to the rectory. It was late and dark when they reached the street. Sangster left Patrick and Roxy in a doorway together—fully realizing the irony of what he was doing—to check the street for Frankie Trigger. When he was satisfied that the hitman was not around, he returned to the doorway, discovering that both were still alive.

"Father Patrick!" Mrs. Cox exclaimed when they walked in. "Are you back? Are you all right?"

"I'm fine, Mrs. Cox," he said.

She stared at him a few moments, then said, "You're far from fine, but far be it for me to call a priest a liar. Are you hungry?" She didn't wait for an answer. "I'll make you something." She went to the kitchen without bothering to speak to Sangster or Roxy.

"What brings you back here?" Burke asked. "I know it ain't over."

"No, not yet," Sangster said, "but I have some ideas."

"Can you share?"

"Let's go into the sitting room," Sangster said.

"Can I come?" Roxy asked.

"Yes," Sangster said. "I insist. I want to keep an eye on you."

"What about food?" Roxy asked.

"Don't worry," Burke said. "Mrs. Cox will bring out enough for everybody."

They went into the sitting room adjacent to the front entryway and Sangster told Burke what had been going on.

"She did what?" Burke blurted, when Sangster got to the part about Roxy pulling her gun.

She had the good sense to avert her eyes.

"Don't worry," Sangster said, "we've sorted things out. She's not going to try that again."

"Are you sure?"

"Yes!" Sangster said. "Let me tell you the rest."

Burke listened to the rest without interrupting, until Sangster was finished.

"How are you gonna get Telemaco to go along with this?" the ex-sheriff asked.

"By giving him his killer," Sangster said.

"Ahhh," Burke said, "that'll make him happy."

"It won't make Frankie Trigger very happy," Roxy pointed out.

"So you'll give him Frankie Trigger," Burke said, "he'll report Father Patrick as dead, and then...what? What does Patrick do?"

"Patrick's thinking about leaving the church," Sangster said, lowering his voice, "and New Orleans. At least this way when he does it, he won't be on the run."

"And Roxy takes the credit?"

"Right."

Burke sat back in his chair.

"I suppose if it works, everybody comes out ahead," he said. "Even Jimmy Abbatello. He'll put his demons to bed."

"Right."

Patrick stuck his head into the room and said, "Who's hungry?"

SIXTY-ONE

Sangster called Detective Telemaco and arranged to meet him in Jackson Square the next afternoon. Then he had to decide what to do with Patrick and Roxy. He left them at the table, picking over what was left of the small feast Mrs. Cox had prepared and took Burke into the sitting room.

"I've got to keep Roxy with me," he said.

"You don't trust her."

"I don't think she'll try to kill Patrick again," he said. "I think I've got her convinced to go along with this plan, but...no, I don't fully trust her."

"So whatta you want to do with Patrick?"

"I could leave him here," Sangster said. "I'm pretty sure Frankie Trigger wasn't outside when we got here. And he's been here already looking for Patrick. He's probably convinced I had him hidden somewhere else."

"Which you did."

"So maybe he wouldn't suspect that I'd bring him back here."

"Well," Burke said, "I've got my gun." He held his hand up to keep Sangster from speaking. "I know I'm no match for the best hitman in the business, but Patrick and I can stay alert. Frankie won't sneak in here. And if he comes to the door—" Burke shrugged. "—I'll shoot 'im."

Sangster thought it over for a few moments, then said, "Yeah, okay. Let him sleep in his own bed after being out in the bayou. Besides, he's got some heavy thinking to do."

"Is he really considering leaving the priesthood?"

"I think he is."

"Why?"

"Something about a crisis of faith he had after meeting Houngan Harry out in the bayou."

"So seein' how Houngan Henry dealt with Papa Legba is makin' him have second thoughts about God or the Catholic Church?"

"I don't know," Sangster said, "and how can I, if he doesn't?"

"Gotcha," Burke said. "So, you and Roxy head out and I'll lock the doors and windows. We'll see ya some time tomorrow."

"I'll call."

"You do that."

They went back to the dining room.

When Sangster and Roxy got back to his house—sure that they hadn't been followed and that no one had been outside the church or Sangster's house—Roxy asked, "So what's the sleepin' arrangements, big boy?"

"You take my bed," he said, "I'll be on the sofa."

"That's how it's gonna be?"

"That's how it's going to be."

She made a face, then shrugged and said, "Well, I don't wanna take your bed. Why don't you give me the sofa?"

"Because I want you to have to go by me if you try to leave."

"You don't trust me," she said.

"Not so much."

"You know," she said, stripping her T-shirt over her head so that she was standing there in a tiny bra, "you'd be able to keep an eye on me better if we slept in the same bed." She walked to the stairs. "I'm just sayin'." And went up.

Sangster watched until she was out of sight, then said, "Oh, what the hell," and followed her.

Just under an hour later Roxy rolled onto her back and stared at the ceiling.

"Wow," she said. "That was better now that we know the rules, wasn't it?"

"You mean because this time you weren't trying to convince me I was irresistible?" Sangster asked.

"Hey," she said, "I told you last time I just wanted to fuck. It's the same this time. It was just a little more...well, honest."

Sangster was also lying on his back. They were both glistening with sweat.

"Speakin' of bein' honest," she asked, "what's with you and the priest?"

"We're friends...sort of."

"Why would you be friends with a priest?" she asked. "Doesn't that seem kind of odd?"

He turned his head and looked at her.

"You want honest?"

"Sure."

"I woke up one day and realized I had a soul."

"Really?"

"Do you have a soul?"

"I—well, I suppose so," she said. "Doesn't everybody?"

"No," he said. "I never did. That's why I was so good at what I did."

"Killin'?"

He nodded.

"So…wait." She propped herself up and really stared at him. His eyes were caught by all the freckles on her shoulders. "Are you tellin' me that to be a good contract killer I can't have a soul?"

"I'm telling you that's what made me a good killer," he replied. "I don't know what'll make you a good one or if you'll ever be a good one."

"So then…how did that feel, suddenly wakin' up and realizing you had a soul?"

"It was…unnerving," he said. "I thought about all the people I killed. I'd never done that before."

"All of them?" she asked. "You remembered them?"

"Yes."

"So what'd you do?"

"I stopped," he said. "That morning. I gave it up."

"Just like that?" she said. "Cold turkey?"

"Yes."

She frowned at him.

"And you haven't killed anybody since?" she asked. "No, wait…you killed my father last year and some of his men."

"I haven't killed anybody for money since that morning."

"Oh," she said, "so you're not a *hired* killer anymore, but you're still a killer."

"We can't completely change who we are. But I don't kill anyone if I don't have to."

"So that's why you wanna give the cops Frankie Trigger. So you don't have to kill him."

"Yes."

"Then let me have him."

"If I do that," he said, "the police won't get their killer and Jimmy Abbatello will still be looking for Patrick."

"Oh."

"Besides," he said, "he'll probably kill you. You're not ready for him."

He thought she was going to protest, but she simply laid down on her back and said, "Maybe you're right. But then again...are you? You've been out of the game for a while."

"Yes, I have," he said.

Which really didn't answer her question.

SIXTY-TWO

Sangster and Roxy arrived in Jackson Square before Detective Telemaco. He took her to one of the corner restaurants and put her at an inside table, near a window.

"Why not outside?" she asked.

"I want to see you," he said, "but I don't necessarily want anyone else to."

"You mean the detective," she said. "He only saw me once, that night at your house."

"He'd remember," Sangster said. He took a menu and set it in front of her. "Order anything you want, on me."

Sangster went out to the square and watched the street performers until Telemaco arrived.

"I was hopin' this was gonna be lunch," the detective said, "on you."

Sangster pointed and asked, "How about a Lucky Dog?"

"That's a start," Telemaco said.

They walked to the Lucky Dog cart and each ordered one and a soda. Sangster watched the detective cover his with mustard, relish and green peppers.

They walked over to the low wall that surrounded the park, against which artists propped their canvases. They examined some of them.

"Wanna stroll?" Telemaco asked.

Sangster stole a look at the window of the restaurant where Roxy was sitting.

"I'd rather just stand here," he said.

"Fine," Telemaco said. "What's on your mind? You said on the phone this had to do with the murder of Vincent Napoli."

"Yeah," Sangster said, "I can give you his killer."

"Is that a fact?" Telemaco swallowed his mouthful of hot dog. "Who is it?"

"Do you know the name Frankie Trigger?"

Telemaco was about to bite into his dog again but stopped short at the sound of that name.

"Top hitman for the east coast families," he said.

"Right."

"And you're sayin' he was here?" Telemaco said. "Killin' Napoli?"

"That's right."

"Why?"

"Look," Sangster said, "I promised to keep this to myself, but the only way I can get you to understand is to give you the full story."

Telemaco stuffed the last of his lunch into his mouth, chewed, swallowed and said, "If that's the case I'm gonna need another dog."

Once Telemaco was armed with another Lucky Dog, Sangster told him the whole story about Father Patrick and Jimmy Abbatello's son.

"And he was cleared?" Telemaco asked.

"Yes, but he was reassigned, several times, to keep Abbatello from him."

"So Abbatello sent Frankie Trigger out to kill Father Patrick. What's this got to do with Vinny Nap?"

"Father Patrick recognized Vinny Nap one day here in Jackson Square," Sangster said. "It stands to reason Vinny Nap also spotted him. He probably called Jimmy Abbatello and told him. Abbatello then sent in Frankie Trigger."

"But why kill Nap?"

Sangster shrugged. "Probably something personal. Jimmy's kind of...unhinged when it comes to his son's death."

"How do you know that?"

Sangster hesitated, then said, "I met him."

"That's interestin'," the detective said. "When?"

"Last week."

"You went to Philly?"

"Father Patrick came to me and asked for my help."

"And what did you do?"

"I went to see Abbatello, pretending to be a hitman."

"Pretending."

"That's right."

Telemaco nodded. He knew Sangster had a dark past, but didn't know what it was, exactly. But the events that had taken place in Vegas the year before certainly indicated that he was no virgin when it came to violence.

"Go on."

"He told me it would be between me and Frankie Trigger," Sangster said. "Whichever one of us got Father Patrick would collect the fee."

"Would you testify to that in court?"

"No."

Telemaco nodded. "Go on."

"Frankie killed Vinny," Sangster said, "and he wants to kill Patrick."

"And what do you want to do?"

"I want to give you Frankie Trigger for Vinny Nap's killer," Sangster said.

"And what do you want in return?"

"I want to make it look like Father Patrick is dead."

"Killed my Frankie Trigger?" Telemaco said. "I can't do that. I can arrest him for Vinny Nap if you prove it to me, but I can't frame him for a murder that didn't even happen."

"No," Sangster said, "I want Patrick's death to look unsolved."

"Oh, I get it," Telemaco said. "You're gonna tell Jimmy you killed him, and collect the fee."

"No," Sangster said, "not me."

"Who, then?" Telemaco asked. "Your girl? She's been sittin' real still in that restaurant window. Hasn't moved a muscle in a while."

"What?"

Sangster looked over at the window and saw what Telemaco meant. Roxy was still in her seat, didn't look like she'd moved at all.

"Ah, shit!" he said, and started running.

"Stark! Wait—" Telemaco started running behind him.

Sangster ran into the restaurant, past two startled patrons and one waitress, and rushed to the window table. Roxy's eyes were open, but she was dead.

SIXTY-THREE

Telemaco rushed Sangster out of the restaurant, along with all the patrons and employees. Then he called for his partner, forensics, the medical examiners and other responders to a homicide scene.

A crowd gathered in Jackson Square, which the police kept back from the restaurant with yellow tape. Sangster was allowed to sit at a table within the taped off area. While seated there he spotted a small hole in the window that Roxy had been seated in front of.

After an hour Telemaco came over and sat with Sangster. From a distance, his partner, Williams, was casting disapproving glances their way.

"What've you got?" Sangster asked.

"She was shot in the temple," Telemaco said.

"The hole in the window?"

"Yeah," the detective said. "It looks like somebody shot her from outside."

"And nobody heard a thing?"

"The gun must have been silenced," Telemaco said, "and the caliber used was small, probably twenty-two or twenty-five. It went through the window cleanly without causing any cracking of the glass."

"Somebody knew what they were doing," Sangster said.

"Like a hitman?"

"Jesus," Sangster said, "he killed her while I was standing out here with you. He probably just walked by and shot her when we weren't looking."

Telemaco sat back and took a deep breath.

"This is on me," Sangster said.

"On me as much as you," Telemaco said, "maybe more. You were facing me. I was facing this restaurant. I looked over here at her from time to time. People were walking by. I might even have seen him and not known it."

"But why?" Sangster asked. "Why kill her?"

"Have you had dealings with him?" Telemaco asked. "Conversations?"

"Just one."

"And what was said?"

"We said that we each knew who the other was."

"Then," Telemaco said, "he might have been sending you a message."

"Yeah," Sangster said, "a message."

"Does she have any family?" Telemaco asked.

"No."

"Nobody to notify?"

"Just me," Sangster said. "I'm the only person she knew in town."

"We'll take her to the morgue," Telemaco said. "I'll be assigned to the case."

"Good."

"Do you know where Frankie Trigger is stayin'?"

"Yes," Sangster said. "I doubt he's there anymore."

"You're sayin' you can hand me Frankie Trigger for killing Vinny Nap."

"Yes."

"Are you satisfied that he killed the girl?"

"Yes."

"Then I want him for that, too."

"Okay."

"How are you gonna do this?"

"You don't want to know."

Telemaco took a deep breath, then leaned forward in his chair.

"Am I gonna get him alive?"

Sangster didn't answer right away.

"Stark?"

"Is that something I have to promise?" Sangster asked.

SIXTY-FOUR

Sangster remained in Jackson Square until the medical examiner had removed Roxy's body. Then he made sure they had his name—Stark—and his address in Algiers, and assuring them he'd be responsible for the body when it was released.

He then drove back to Algiers and the rectory, where he informed Burke, Patrick and Mrs. Cox what had happened to Roxy.

"Oh my God," Mrs. Cox said, making the sign of the cross. "That poor girl." She withdrew to the kitchen.

Sangster did not think it was odd that it was the housekeeper who executed the sign of the cross, not the priest. Especially with what he knew about Patrick's inner turmoil.

"I'm so sorry," Burke said. "What did Telemaco say?"

"He believes it was Frankie Trigger sending me a message," Sangster said.

"So he's gonna go along with your plan?"

"Yes."

"But..." Patrick said.

They both looked at him.

"I'm sorry, but...the plan was for her to take credit for killing me," he said. "What do we do now?"

"We adjust," Sangster said. "If Telemaco can put

Frankie away, I think Jimmy Abbatello's going to be very happy that he doesn't have to pay the man for killing you."

"So you're gonna make him think Frankie killed me."

"I'm going to let him draw his own conclusion."

"Why don't you just take the credit?" Patrick asked.

"I'm not going back to Philly to see Jimmy," Sangster said. "We're going to end this here in New Orleans, and then you can do what you want."

"I haven't decided yet what I want to do," Patrick admitted."

"Well," Sangster said. "I can only help you with dying. After that you're on your own."

Mrs. Cox did what she always did with stress and trouble—she fed it. Once the table was loaded with food Sangster, Burke and Patrick sat down.

"What's your plan?" Burke asked, while they ate.

"I don't think I have to have a plan," Sangster said.

"What do you mean?" Patrick asked.

"Frankie Trigger killed Roxy," he said. "If it was a message to me, then he has a plan. All I have to do is wait for him to call."

"That could take a long time," Patrick said.

"No," Sangster said, "he wants to get this done. He took a big chance killing Roxy right there in Jackson Square. He's ready to make a big move."

"To kill me?" Patrick said.

"To kill you, me, and anybody else who's with me," Sangster said. He looked at the ex-sheriff. "Burke, you have to go home and sit this one out."

"No way."

"Yes, you have to," Sangster said. "Frankie won't hesitate to kill you. And you'll have to take Mrs. Cox with you."

"Where?" she asked, coming out of the kitchen.

"You need to go and stay at Sheriff Burke's house for a while," Sangster said. "Until this is over."

"Isn't it safer here?"

"No," Sangster said. "He knows about this place, but he doesn't know where Burke lives."

"I repeat," Mrs. Cox said, looking at Burke, "isn't this safer?"

"He got in once, right?" Sangster asked.

Mrs. Cox grew quiet.

"I could take her to Polly's," Burke offered. "She might feel...safer."

"Polly?" Mrs. Cox said.

"My..."

"His..."

"...lady friend."

"...cleaning lady."

Sangster and Burke looked at each other.

"Which is it?" she asked.

"Both," Burke said.

"Does she have room?" Mrs. Cox asked.

"She has three kids," Burke said, "but they're in Jamaica right now."

"All right, then," she said. "I'll pack a bag."

Burke nodded. She turned and went to her room.

"I'll clean-up for her," Burke said, and started clearing the table.

Sangster and Patrick went back into the front sitting room.

"Is this gonna work?" Patrick asked.

"It has to," Sangster said. "If it doesn't, we'll both have to go on the run."

"Really?"

"What?"

"I was under the impression that we both already were," the priest said.

SIXTY-FIVE

They all left the rectory together, keeping a sharp eye out for Frankie Trigger. They drove Mrs. Cox to Polly's house. Burke got out of the car to walk her in.

"I'll be right back," he said to Sangster, who was driving.

"Right."

As Polly admitted Mrs. Cox and Burke to her house Sangster started the engine.

"What are you doin'?" Patrick asked.

"Making sure Burke stays safe," he said, driving away.

Patrick turned in his seat to look back at Polly's house. He saw Burke come out the door and stand looking after them with his hands on his hips.

"Sheriff Burke's not happy."

"He'll get over it," Sangster said, "because he'll still be alive."

Sangster drove to his house and left Patrick on the front porch while he went inside.

"Where are we goin'?" Patrick asked, as Sangster came out.

"I'm not sure," Sangster said. "I think that's going to be up to Frankie. I'm still expecting his call."

"And when he calls? What's he gonna want?"

"That's easy," Sangster said. "He's going to want you, and me."

"And that's what we're gonna give him, right?"

"That's what it's going to look like we're giving him," Sangster said.

Patrick sat back in his chair, eyed the chess set on the table in front of him.

"Are we gonna wait here?" he asked.

"No," Sangster said. "I don't want to make it too easy for Frankie to find us. And besides, Burke may look for us here. I don't want him finding us, either. Come on."

They went back down the walk to the street and got into Sangster's car.

"Where to?" Patrick asked.

"I don't—" At that point the cell phone in Sangster's pocket went off. "Maybe this will tell us.

But it wasn't Frankie. It was Detective Telemaco. Sangster had given him the phone number.

"Hello."

"Stark? Telemaco here."

"What's up?"

"Frankie Trigger," the detective said. "He checked out of that B&B he was in."

"That's not a surprise."

"Have you heard from him?"

"No."

"You'd tell me, right?"

"I would."

"How do you expect him to contact you?"

"I expect him to be resourceful," Sangster said.

"Then I'll just wait to hear from you."

"You will?"

"That's what you want me to do, ain't it?"

"Yeah, it is."

"Let's just hope it doesn't take too long."

Sangster broke the contact.

"What was that about?"

"Nothing we didn't already know," Sangster said. "Frankie checked out of his B&B. The cops have no idea where he is."

"And neither do we," Patrick said. "Why do I feel like I've got a bullseye on my back? And he's out there takin'?"

"Well, he's out there," Sangster said. "That much is true."

SIXTY-SIX

As Sangster drove off the ferry, he turned and started driving up Canal Street.

"Something just occurred to me," he said.

"What's that?" Patrick asked.

"We can't find Frankie and he can't find us."

"So, that's bad?" Patrick asked. "If he can't find us, why don't we just keep goin'?"

"What about the church?" Sangster asked.

"I've decided I'm leavin'," Patrick said.

"Have you told them?"

"No."

"Don't you have to resign, or something?"

"Usually," Patrick said, "but since I'm tryin' to stay alive, I thought I'd just go."

"They'll be worried," Sangster said, "Mrs. Cox, the Monsignor—"

"They'll get over it." Patrick looked at him. "Besides, didn't you do somethin' like that at one time?"

"Maybe," Sangster said, "but I didn't have anyone to say goodbye to."

"What about now?"

"If I had to go, I'd go," Sangster said.

"Then why don't we?"

"Look," Sangster said, "how about I let you off on

the corner. You can take off and even I won't know where you are."

Patrick fidgeted in his seat.

"I might still run into Frankie Trigger," Patrick said. "Or someone else lookin' to connect."

"That's true."

"Well then…what were you thinkin'?"

"It seems to me Frankie likes Jackson Square."

"Why would he go back there after he killed Roxy?"

"Because he's arrogant," Sangster said, "and because nobody saw him do it and nobody can prove it."

"Still…why go there?"

"So I can find him."

"Okay," Patrick said, frustrated, "I guess I'm just not understandin' this kind of thinkin'. He's lookin' for me. He doesn't know we're together. He thinks you're also lookin' for me to kill me."

"True," Sangster said, "we hope."

"So why would he wait right out there in the open for you to find him?" Patrick asked. "Wouldn't he be afraid you'd kill him?"

"I don't have any reason to kill him," Sangster said. "There's no profit in it."

"So what are you gonna do?"

"I'm going to leave you somewhere, then go and check Jackson Square."

"And if he's there?"

"I'll have to convince him that I killed you," Sangster said, "and then get him to admit to killing Vinny Nap and Roxy."

"Why would he do that?"

"Same reason I gave you before," Sangster said. "Arrogance."

"And then you'll have him arrested?"

"First I need him to call his buddy Jimmy and tell him you're dead."

"Won't he expect you to do that?"

"Yeah, he would," Sangster said. "I'm going to have to come up with a reason for him to do it."

"This sounds like a lot of ifs and buts to me," Patrick said, shaking his head.

"True enough."

"Where are you gonna leave me?"

"I'm thinking."

Sangster decided the best thing to do with Patrick was hide him in plain sight. He wasn't wearing his collar, so he wouldn't stand out.

He drove outside of the French Quarter to the downtown area and left Patrick off in front of a small café.

"Go in and have something to eat," he said. "Stay away from the window."

"How long do I stay here?"

"Until I come and get you," Sangster said.

"W-what if Frankie kills you?"

"If I don't come and get you," Sangster said, "Burke or Telemaco will."

Patrick opened his door, then looked back at Sangster.

"Are you sure about this?"

"I'm not sure about any of this," Sangster said.

"That doesn't fill me with a lot of confidence."

"Me, neither."

"Sangster—"

"Go, Patrick. This is either going to all be over or

you can just go ahead and take off, like you want to."

"And look over my shoulder for the rest of my life."

"I'd say have faith," Sangster said, "but…"

"Yeah," Patrick said, and got out of the car.

SIXTY-SEVEN

Sangster had a few things to do before going to Jackson Square. When he walked into the area things were in place. He had Roxy's gun in his jacket pocket, although his fervent hope was that he wouldn't have to use it.

Frankie Trigger was, indeed, there, and his arrogance was on full display as he was seated at a table in front of the very restaurant Roxy had been in when he killed her.

"You're a hard man to find," Frankie said.

"So why come here?"

"Seems like everybody comes through here sooner or later. This is the last place I saw you," Frankie said. "You were with a cop."

Sangster sat across from him.

"You killed Roxy," Sangster said.

"What were you doin' with a cop?"

"What do you ever do with a cop?" Sangster replied. "I was answering questions."

"About what?"

"They're still trying to find out who killed Vinny Nap," Sangster said. "Although you and I know who did."

"Do we?"

"And you killed Roxy," Sangster said, again.

"Did I?"

"Right here, with a cop in the Square," Sangster said. He saw that the window had been replaced. "That takes a lot of balls, Frankie."

A waitress came out and for the purpose of appearances they each ordered an Abita beer.

"What about the priest?" Frankie asked.

"Oh him," Sangster said. "He's dead."

"You killed him?"

"I did."

"Did you call Jimmy Abbatello?"

"I thought I'd let you deliver the news."

Frankie looked surprised.

"Why would you let me do that?" he asked. "What if I tell him I killed him?"

"I'd have to call you a liar," Sangster said, "but in spite of the fact that you're a lot of things, I don't think you're a liar."

Frankie frowned.

"How do I know you're tellin' me the truth?"

Sangster took Patrick's collar from his pocket and dropped it on the table.

"That doesn't prove anythin'."

"Then I guess you'll have to decide whether or not I'm a liar."

The waitress came and set their beers down. Frankie Trigger picked up his bottle and while he drank, his eyes raked the Square. As usual it was alive with people—both spectators and performers.

Sangster sipped his beer and set the bottle down.

"You're carryin' today," Frankie said, holding his bottle in his left hand.

"Just playing it safe."

"You bring any friends with you?"

"I don't have any friends?"

"What about that ex-sheriff?"

"He's my neighbor."

"Uh-huh."

"You know men like you and me don't make friends," Sangster said.

"Men like you and me," Frankie said, "We coulda *been* friends?"

"Sure," Sangster said, "we'll take in a ballgame together."

Frankie grinned and drank from his beer.

"So you want me to believe you've closed out this contract," he said.

"I don't care if you believe it or not," Sangster said. "I'm just telling you that we're not working against each other anymore—I mean, as far as I'm concerned."

"What if you're just tryin' to get me to leave New Orleans, givin' you a clear field?"

"Like I said," Sangster replied, "you're going to have to decide if I'm a liar or not."

"You know," Frankie said, "we kill people, you and me. How can lying be any worse than that?"

"You think what you do is bad?"

"Bad, evil," Frankie said. "Who knows? What do you think?"

"I didn't used to think about it at all," Sangster said. "I just did it."

"That's what we have to do," Frankie said. "To be what we are, we just have to do it. Otherwise, we'd never be able to live with it."

To be what he once was, Sangster wanted to say, and was no longer.

"Frankie," he said, "if you believe that, then how can you—"

"Whoa," Frankie said, "stop right there, pal. This is not a come-to-Jesus meetin'. I am what I am, and I have no second thoughts about it. Not this far into the game."

"No," Sangster said, "I suppose not."

"All right, then." Frankie Trigger got to his feet. "I guess you killed the priest. Go to Jimmy and collect your money." He turned to walk away.

"What are you going to do?"

"Move on to the next job," Frankie said, "the next contract."

"Wait!"

Frankie turned back.

"If you only kill under contract, why kill Vinny Nap?"

"Jimmy wanted him gone," Frankie said. "That was an extra job I did for him."

"And Roxy? Why her?"

"You know," Frankie said, "I'm not really sure about that one. I think I did it..." He shrugged. "...just to send a message. I guess I figured maybe you'd back off."

"You figured wrong."

"So, what? We gonna throw down right here? In front of all these people?"

Sangster stood up. He knew Frankie Trigger would get his gun out of his holster well before he could get Roxy's gun from his pocket. So he kept his hand away from the gun, reached up and tugged at his ear.

* * *

Across the Square, in the window of another restaurant, Detective Telemaco tapped a uniformed policeman on the shoulder and said, "Okay, put it down."

The cop set down the shotgun mike he had been holding and aiming across the way at Sangster and Frankie Trigger.

Telemaco put his radio to his lips and said, "Let's do it. Move in!"

SIXTY-EIGHT

Frankie saw the cops coming from different points in the Square toward him. He looked at Sangster.

"Why would you do this?" he asked. "We're alike."

"We used to be alike," Sangster said. "We're not, anymore."

"Wait a minute," Frankie said, as the truth dawned on him. "You don't kill anymore."

Sangster said nothing.

"So you didn't kill the priest and you won't kill me."

Frankie looked at the cops again, easily half a dozen men with guns, then turned and looked through the window into the restaurant. In the table previously occupied by Roxy was a mother, father and small boy, eating their lunch. Frankie reached out and touched his finger to the spot he'd fired through to kill Roxy.

"If they don't stop comin'," he said, "I'll kill the boy."

"Frankie—"

"Then the mother and father."

"Frankie—"

"Better hold them back, Sangster," Frankie said. His gun was in a shoulder holster beneath his jacket. He put his hand on the butt.

Sangster looked at the cops, being led my Telemaco, as they came closer.

"Sangster—" Frankie said.

While Frankie was once again watching the cops, he started to draw his gun to fulfill his threat to the family behind the window.

Sangster yanked Roxy's gun from his jacket pocket and shot Frankie Trigger through the heart.

Hours later the door to the interrogation room opened and Telemaco walked in.

"About time," Sangster said.

Telemaco put a bottle of water in front of Sangster and sat across from him. Sangster opened the bottle and drank gratefully. He'd been sitting in that room for two hours.

"Where's your partner? Behind the mirror?"

"It's just you and me, Stark," Telemaco said. "And believe me, it wasn't easy. You shot Frankie Trigger in front of six cops."

"I didn't have a choice," Sangster said. "I told you that."

"I know," Telemaco said. "He was gonna shoot a kid."

"Right through the window like he did Roxy," Sangster said.

"I believe you," the detective said. "That's the only reason you're in this room and not in a cell right now."

"And how much longer do I have to stay in this room?" Sangster asked.

"I had to do a lot of talkin'," Telemaco said, "but not too much longer."

"Talking about what?"

"Well, there are some people in the department who want you arrested."

"Your partner?"

"For one, but also my immediate superiors. They really aren't happy with gunplay in Jackson Square. They think it sends a negative message to the tourists."

"So would shooting kids in Jackson Square," Sangster said. "Not to mention Roxy."

"I made that point," Telemaco said. "I convinced them that if Trigger had shot that boy, things would've been a lot worse."

"So I'm in the clear, then?"

"We checked your prints, Stark," Telemaco said. "Turns out you're not in the system."

Sangster didn't say a word. He'd made sure, over the years, that he never made it into the system.

"My boss wonders why?"

"Maybe I'm clean," Sangster said.

"Well," Telemaco said, sitting back in his chair, "you and I both know that's not true."

"So what's your boss want to do about it?"

"He wants me to keep an eye on you," Telemaco said. "A close eye. Those are my orders."

"Well," Sangster said, "you know where to find me."

"Yeah, I do," Telemaco said. "I'm just warnin' you, Stark—or whatever your name really is. Yeah, I'm not stupid."

"I never thought you were."

"You can go."

Sangster stood up and left.

* * *

When he picked up Patrick, the priest was in a panic.

"I thought you were dead," he said, getting into the front seat. "What happened?"

"Frankie's dead," Sangster said.

"You killed him?"

"I didn't have a choice."

"What happened?"

Sangster started the car and headed for the ferry as he told the story to Father Patrick.

"So you killed him in front of a half a dozen policemen?"

"And Telemaco."

"Were they gonna arrest you?"

"Apparently everybody but Telemaco wanted to," Sangster said. "He talked them out of it."

"That's a good friend to have."

"We're not exactly friends."

"He sure sounds like a friend."

They drove in silence, until they were on the ferry heading for Algiers. They chose to remain in the car during the ride.

"So what now?" Patrick asked.

"I'll have to talk to Jimmy and convince him that you're dead."

"Can you do that?"

"I think so," Sangster said. "It'll be pretty easy to prove to him that Frankie's dead. Once he knows I killed Frankie, I think he'll believe I killed you."

"So then you collect on the contract."

"I suppose I'll have to," Sangster said. "It would look pretty suspicious if I said no."

"What will you do with the money?"

"I don't know," Sangster said. "I guess I'll give it to charity. Or put it in the poor box."

There was a short silence, and then Patrick said, "I have an idea what you could do with the money."

EPILOGUE

Sangster drank his coffee and stared at the chess problem in front of him. As ex-Sheriff Burke came up the walk, Sangster shifted his attention from the chessboard.

"Are you talking to me now?'

"You did what you thought you had to do," Burke said. "I'm okay with it now."

"Finally. It's only been a week."

Burke sat across from him. He was holding a coffee mug of his own.

"Patrick must be well into the wind now with that money you gave him. Or rather, that Jimmy Abbatello gave him. Kind of ironic, don't you think?"

"I thought that when Patrick told me the idea."

"Are we sure Abbatello believes he's dead?"

"Fairly sure."

"Poor Patrick," Burke said. "He's completely lost his faith. He's more lost than he ever was."

"I sympathize with him," Sangster said. "Or is the word 'empathize?'"

"Watching a Catholic priest lose his faith sure as hell couldn't have helped you any."

"It didn't," Sangster said. "But I'm not all that sure it really matters, anymore."

"Whataya mean?"

"I think I've been spending too much time trying to figure out what to do with a soul," Sangster said. "I think maybe it should be enough just to know I have one."

"So then you're just as confused as the rest of us," Burke said.

"Pretty much."

"What about your friend Telemaco?"

"He's keeping tabs on me," Sangster said.

"You gonna try to keep outta trouble?"

"Isn't that what I've done since I moved here?"

Burke looked into his coffee cup.

"Set up the board. I'm gonna get a refill."

"Me, too," Sangster said, handing the ex-lawman his mug.

As Burke went into the house for coffee refills, Sangster sat back in his chair and looked out at the street. The contract money had been delivered to him by Joseph Maniscalco earlier in the week, and then he'd handed it to Patrick.

He'd met Maniscalco in Louis Armstrong Airport, in the Delta Airlines Sky Club.

"Not staying?" Sangster asked.

"In New Orleans? Not a chance," Maniscalco said. "I'm catchin' the next flight back to Philly in fifteen minutes." He passed Sangster an envelope, which the ex-hitman tucked into his jacket. "You're not gonna count it?"

"I trust you."

"Jimmy says he might need you again, now that Frankie Trigger is out of the picture.

"I don't think so."

"Why not?"

"I'm out of the business," Sangster said. "This was my last job."

"You better count it after all," Maniscalco said. "You didn't get paid that much."

"Tell Jimmy thanks but no thanks."

"Well, you never know," Maniscalco said. "We know where you are."

Not quite, Sangster said, which was one of the reasons the meeting was taking place at the airport.

"That's my flight," Maniscalco said, hearing an announcement Sangster hadn't heard. "See ya, kid."

As the man walked away Sangster was determined never to see him or his boss again.

As Burke came out with the mugs Sangster finished setting up the chess pieces and accepted his coffee.

"What's next?" Burke asked.

"I'm thinking about leaving."

"Algiers?"

"Louisiana, period."

"Why?"

"Everybody thinks they know where they can find me," he said. "Telemaco is supposed to keep an eye on me, Jimmy Abbatello wants to use me again—"

"He can't find you out here."

"Maybe not."

"If you go," Burke said, "I won't have anybody to play chess with."

"That's your main concern?"

"Hey," Burke said, "I'm a selfish old bastard."

Sangster sipped his coffee and reached out for his queen's pawn. He'd set himself up with white and Burke with black.

"Okay," he said, moving the pawn, "I'll give it some more thought."

AUTHOR'S NOTE

Certain liberties were taken with some depictions of New Orleans—like some of its streets, shops, and bayous. If anyone detects what they think are errors, please know that they were made for reasons.

ROBERT J. RANDISI is the author of the "Miles Jacoby," "Nick Delvecchio," "Gil & Claire Hunt," "Dennis McQueen," "Joe Keough," "The Rat Pack," "Jimmy Spain Poker," and "Housesitting Detective" mystery series'. He is the editor of over 30 anthologies. All told he is the author of over 650 novels.

He is the founder of the Private Eye Writers of America, the creator of the Shamus Award, the co-founder of Mystery Scene Magazine.

OTHER TITLES FROM DOWN AND OUT BOOKS

See www.DownAndOutBooks.com for complete list

By J.L. Abramo
Chasing Charlie Chan
Circling the Runway
Brooklyn Justice
Coney Island Avenue (*)

By Trey R. Barker
Exit Blood
Death is Not Forever
No Harder Prison

By Eric Beetner
and Frank Zafiro
The Backlist
The Shortlist

By Angel Luis Colón
No Happy Endings
Meat City on Fire (*)

By Shawn Corridan
and Gary Waid
Gitmo (*)

By Frank De Blase
Pine Box for a Pin-Up
Busted Valentines
A Cougar's Kiss

By Les Edgerton
The Genuine, Imitation,
Plastic Kidnapping
Lagniappe (*)

By Danny Gardner
A Negro and an Ofay (*)

By Jack Getze
Big Mojo
Big Shoes
Colonel Maggie & the Black
Kachina

By Richard Godwin
Wrong Crowd
Buffalo and Sour Mash
Crystal on Electric Acetate (*)

By Jeffery Hess
Beachhead
Cold War Canoe Club (*)

By Matt Hilton
Rules of Honor
The Lawless Kind
The Devil's Anvil
No Safe Place

By Lawrence Kelter
and Frank Zafiro
The Last Collar

By Lawrence Kelter
Back to Brooklyn (*)

(*)—Coming Soon

www.ingramcontent.com/pod-product-compliance
Lightning Source LLC
Chambersburg PA
CBHW051650180726
48284CB00006B/1946